THE BODYGUARD

A Curvy Girl MC Romance

Nichole Rose

Kindle Edition

Copyright © 2022 by Nichole Rose

Cover by Yoly at Cormar Covers

CONTENTS

DEDICATION

To Kat Canganelli – Readers like you are the reason I do what I do. Thank you for giving my imagination a small place in your life.

About the Book

Even giants fall...and the last brother standing will fall like a ton of bricks when he meets the feisty curvy girl meant to complete him.

Cormac "Giant" Carmichael

For the last year and a half, I've watched my MC brothers drop like flies.

I almost gave up on finding my one.

And then my dad called in a favor for a friend of a friend.

His daughter is in trouble and needs my help.

They forgot to mention that she's a fiery little goddess.

Bella Sterling would rather set me on fire and watch me burn than let me watch her back.

The harder she fights, the more confident I am that she's my one.

This curvy little minx can run, but she can't hide from me.

When the stakes are this high, I *always* get what I want.

And I want her. Forever.

Bella Sterling

Someone explain how I witnessed a crime and ended up a prisoner.

Because it doesn't make any sense to me, but that's my life anyway.

My parents have sentenced me to hide out in Silver Spoon Falls.

Worse, I have a hulking giant breathing down my neck.

He keeps claiming that I belong to him.

And some crazy part of me aches to believe him.

Especially when he turns that sexy pirate's smile on me.

But my life—and my twin—is in Tennessee.

That's where I belong...isn't it?

Chapter One

Giant

"Here," Tate "Hands" Grimes says, sliding a glass of water across the bar to me as soon as I plant my ass on a barstool in the Silver Spoon MC clubhouse. Droplets splash out, pooling on the live edge bar top. "Thought you might want this."

I glance down at it and then up at my MC brother. "Fuck off with that water bullshit. It doesn't even work."

Every brother at the bar turns to look at me in complete shock.

"Jesus Christ." Andreas "Playboy" Romano slumps forward on his barstool beside me, heaving a sigh like I just ruined his night. "Here we go with this shit again."

I shoot him a dirty scowl, not entirely sure how I ended up with an unsympathetic asshole for a best friend. The least he can do is let me wallow in my misery in silence. But no. He's been riding my dick for the last hour. I need nicer friends. Mine are mean to me.

"You don't believe in the water anymore?" Jason "Cash" Montoya, our club prez, asks. All my MC brothers are convinced the water in this town is why they've all fallen in love at the speed of light. He eyes me like I just said I'm moving to the North Pole to take over for St. Nick. No, thank you. Child labor is cruel and unusual, and I'm pretty goddamn certain those elves of his are children. "Since when?"

"Since I found out my parents hate me," I mutter.

"What the fuck?" Finn "Hacker" Taylor rumbles.

"What the fuck?" Hands repeats.

"For fuck's sake, Giant," Andreas growls, throwing up his hands. "That is *not* what they said."

"Uh, I'm pretty fucking certain it is," I disagree, swiping his beer before he can take a drink. I knock it back, draining half the bottle at once. Stealing his shit doesn't help. My life still sucks.

Andreas issues another long-suffering sigh. "They asked you to watch over a friend's daughter for a few weeks. That's *not* the same thing."

I lower the bottle to glare at him. "You ever tried finding your soulmate while another woman is living in your house, fucking up the program?"

"Uh, Autumn lived with me when I found Catriona."

"She's your sister."

"So?"

I take back what I said. I don't need nicer friends. I need smarter friends.

"Hi, my name is Cormac. Would you like to go out with me? Oh, don't mind the chick living in my house. You know, the one I follow everywhere but can't tell you who she is? She's no one important," I say, pursing my lips and batting my eyes until he gets the fucking point. No woman wants to hear some shit like that...and that's precisely what I'd have to tell anyone I dated while this chick, Bella Sterling, lives with me.

A week ago, she witnessed two men murder one of the wealthiest men in Tennessee in cold blood. In the days since, someone has broken into her car and her apartment. Her parents want her out of the state until the murderers are behind bars and she's safe.

Since I run the Texas branch of my family's private security firm, Carmichael Security, I'm the lucky motherfucker they trust with her safety. Normally, I wouldn't balk at taking the job. The girl is twenty-one and scared out of her mind. Nothing pisses me off more than motherfuckers who target women. We've been down that road too damn often over the last year and a half, starting with Cash and his wife, Hadley.

Plus, I'd do just about anything for my parents. But fuck my life. Ever since Damien "Angel" De Angelis met Milly and fell in love, I'm the last brother standing around here. Everyone is happily coupled up and popping out kids like they're single-handedly trying to populate Silver Spoon Falls.

If I have to hear them talk about their sex lives one more goddamn time, I may snap. Not saying I'm not happy for them. I'm thrilled they've all found love. The fuckers deserve it. But I want what they have so badly I can taste it. I've been looking for my one my entire life. Haven't found her yet. And it doesn't look like I'm going to find her anytime soon at this rate.

"I'm going to die alone," I say morosely, glancing down at my cock. "You're doomed to a life of lotion and audio porn."

"You aren't going to die alone," Cash mutters.

"What the fuck is audio porn?" Cowboy asks.

"Ask your wife." Hacker smirks, leaning back against the wall. "I bet she can tell you all about it."

Cowboy scowls as if he doesn't like the sound of this. Whatever though. He's reaping the benefits of the wives' dirty book club. I have to listen to their dirty audiobooks alone. It's not nearly as much fun for me.

"The important question is why this girl needs around-the-clock protection," Jude "Fifth" Despora says quietly. He glances at my brothers and then focuses those serious eyes on me. The man is a lawyer, but I think if Anubis ever gets tired of his gig in the Underworld, Fifth could take over easy. He's a kinky motherfucker when it comes to his wife. I've heard things no man should ever hear. But his moral compass never deviates. Neither do ours. He refuses to let them.

"Remember hearing about the recording label exec who was murdered in Nashville?" I ask.

"Bellamy Hill?"

"She witnessed it."

Rafe "Lynch" Sorraco whistles.

"Jesus Christ," Cash growls. "His dealers killed him."

"Yep," I agree. "That's the rumor."

"How the fuck did she get tangled up in that?" Hands asks, popping the top off a bottle and propping a hip against the bar. His brows furrow. "The last thing we need around the girls and the kids is someone involved in drugs, Giant."

I give him a look. He knows damn well I refuse to work with anyone who isn't clean. I don't care how much money they wave at me or who they are. If they're using, I don't accept them as clients. Trying to keep someone alive in dangerous situations is hard enough. Trying to keep them alive when they're high as a kite and don't fucking listen is next to impossible. There isn't enough money in the world worth that bullshit.

"She was interning for him," I say. "Guess they thought she'd left for the night when they decided to ambush him in the parking deck. They didn't see her in the stairwell until the deed was done."

"Jesus," Fifth mutters.

Cash heaves a sigh, scrubbing a hand down his face. "What do you need?"

"A new job," I mutter. "Mine sucks."

Andreas kicks my barstool.

I huff out a curse. "Fuck. I meet her at the airport tomorrow." Callum, my cousin, is flying her in. His home office is in Nashville, though I don't fucking know why. He spends more time here lately than he does there. "I may need help keeping an eye on her. From the sounds of it, she isn't exactly thrilled to be coming." According to my dad, she called coming here a prison sentence. Her dad, Mac, warned me that she can be a handful. Though how much trouble one little slip of a girl can actually cause, I don't fucking know.

I guess I'll find out tomorrow.

Fuck my life.

If I never give my parents grandchildren, it'll be their own damn fault.

"Yo, man. We have a problem."

I pinch the bridge of my nose, lifting my gaze to look up at the glass ceiling. "The plane landed fifteen minutes ago. How can we possibly already have a problem?" I growl to my cousin, Callum. "You've been through every fucking airport in the south. There's no way you were followed."

"Yeah, that's not the problem."

"Explain," I demand. It's way too late for riddles. Their last flight was delayed, and I've been cooling my heels for three hours. I could be in bed right now, fantasizing about my future wife. I hope she's a curvy little goddess with sugar in her soul.

My ordinarily stoic, level-headed cousin grits out a curse. "As soon as we deplaned, she ducked into the bathroom."

"So go in and get her."

"Tried that. She's not in there. There's a goddamn exit on the other side. She gave me the slip."

"Son of a bitch," I curse, instantly on red alert. Houston International is a maze, with flights to damn near any and everywhere. Mac Sterling will kill me if I lose his daughter before I ever even have her in my possession. And then my dad will bring me back and kill me again. "Get me a fucking photo."

"I swear to God, Cormac, this chick is a menace," Callum mutters. "I'm too young for angina."

"Maybe she just doesn't like you."

He snorts. "Fine. Make your jokes, but don't say I didn't fucking warn you."

I'm suddenly curious as a motherfucker to know what she did to piss in his Cheerios. He's former Special Forces. It takes a hell of a lot to stress him out. But she's managed to do it in all of twenty-four hours. Either she's exactly as bad as her dad said, or Callum is losing his touch.

"Send a photo through," I demand, striding toward the security checkpoint.

"Already did." He pauses. "She shouldn't be hard to spot. Look for a curvy brunette wearing hot pink leggings and a white hoodie. She's deceptively angelic for a fucking menace to society."

"What'd she do to piss you off?"

"Nailed me in the balls with her backpack. And then stomped on my foot."

I bark a laugh, eager as hell to meet this chick now.

"It's not funny," Callum growls. "She has a laptop, a Kindle, textbooks, and about twenty pounds of random shit in that bag. My fucking balls still ache."

I laugh again, drawing attention from passersby. Swear to Christ, I get tired of people staring at me. It's not my fault I didn't stop growing at a normal motherfucker's size. I'm six-eight and over three hundred pounds. I stick out like a sore thumb, attracting attention no matter where the hell I go. It's inconvenient as hell.

"Why'd she nail you in the balls?" I ask, trying to ignore the stares turned in my direction.

"She thought I was staring at her ass."

"Were you?"

"I've got three little sisters who torture me just because they can," he mutters. "Do you think I need a goddamn hellcat to stress me the fuck out all day, every day too? Hell no, I wasn't looking at her ass. I do not need another woman in my life giving me shit to worry about."

"Well, damn. Why don't you tell me how you really feel?"

He grunts and then mumbles an apology, though I'm guessing it's not aimed at me since he tacks a *sweetheart* onto the end, trying to be all smooth and shit. My gaze drifts around baggage claim, my eyes peeled for anyone with a badge who can help a brother out before Bella Sterling dashes off to God only knows where.

My gaze lands on a goddess instead, and my legs stop working. My feet just fucking forget how to move. I trip forward two steps, damn near landing on my face in the middle of a conveyor belt. I catch myself at the last second, not taking my eyes off the brunette beauty.

There are curves, and then there's this girl. She's soft and round in all the right places. Every inch of her screams sex, from her pouty lips to her thick thighs. Even though her hair is piled up on top of her head, little ringlets hang free around her heart-shaped face, framing it. Her pink cheeks and pouty lips make my cock throb. Not even her oversized hoodie hides how her tits bounce with every step she takes. Her leggings cling to her legs, molding to every inch of those thighs.

"What'd you say she's wearing again?" I growl to Callum, eating up the sight of this girl like a fucking blind man seeing color for the first time. Goddamn, she's pretty.

"White hoodie, hot pink leggings," my cousin mutters.

This pretty little thing is Bella Sterling?

"I take back everything I said yesterday."

She's hauling ass across baggage claim like the hounds of hell nip at her heels, casting furtive glances over her shoulder as if she fully expects to see them appear out of the crowd at any moment. I shift my gaze over her shoulder, trying to pinpoint a specific threat, but I don't see anyone out of place. I figure that means she's running from Callum.

Fuck, I think I love her already. I'd run from his crabby ass too.

"About what? What the fuck are you talking about?"

"Never mind. I found our girl. Meet us at baggage claim." I hang up on him before he can ask me any questions and shove my phone into my pocket. Even though she's running as fast as her short legs will carry her, I cut across the two aisles between us, strategically placing myself between her and the doors.

She's so busy looking over her shoulder that she plows right into me.

"Oh!" she cries.

I grab her before she bounces off and lands on her sexy ass on the floor.

"Careful, Mischief," I rumble, biting back a groan as my hands sink into her soft curves. Fuck me running. Either I've been a very good boy, indeed, or I'm going straight to hell in a handbasket because Bella Sterling is the sweetest ride I've ever had my hands on. And I'm pretty goddamn sure the one place I'm not supposed to have said hands is on her perfect little body.

Mac Sterling is going to kill me.

But oh, what a way to go.

CHAPTER TWO

Bella

Either Texans are built different, or I hopped on a plane headed straight to hell. Because I just escaped one giant. And now I've got another one staring at me with a smile that's all pirate. And unlike the other giant, this one doesn't annoy me on sight. He is...wow.

Dark brown hair sweeps across his forehead, overly long and a little unkempt, not as if he's been running his hands through it, but more like he's had it smashed down inside a helmet for a while. There's steel in his gray eyes and a bump on his nose that matches. It's been broken at least once before. But it doesn't detract from how freaking hot he is. If anything, it gives him a wicked, sexy vibe, especially paired with those killer dimples.

I'm not a small girl, but his hands nearly touch where they're wrapped around me. And I've got my head craned all the way back to meet his gaze. He doesn't tower over me. He dwarfs me like the earth swallowing the moon's shadow. He's by far the biggest man I've ever met. And my uncle used to play football professionally, so I've seen big men before now.

I don't even have to ask to know that he's related to the other giant, Callum. I'm guessing that makes him Cormac Carmichael, the man I've been fobbed off on for the foreseeable future. It's a pity, really. Because this man is five-alarm fire hot, and he's doing crazy things to my body. My skin tingles like it's waking up for the very first time, and my stomach flutters and spins.

But I am so not sleeping with the enemy.

And he may not know it yet, but he is the enemy. My dad just *decided* I should come here without even giving me a say, and this man willingly agreed. No one asked my opinion. They chose for me. And I've never much cared for following along obediently.

I bet this is how the Fresh Prince felt. Only...this is probably worse than that. Because at least he had family in Bel-Air. I know no one in Texas, and I'm not running from a fight. I'm hiding from the cowards who murdered my boss in cold blood.

I just want to go home to my twin, Isla, and my life. I want to be there when they catch the men who murdered

Bellamy. Is that so wrong? I liked my boss. Despite what everyone says about him, they're wrong. He was a good, honest man. He wasn't involved in drugs and didn't deserve what happened to him. But I can't do anything about it from Texas.

"My name isn't Mischief," I growl, narrowing my eyes at Cormac. "It's not baby, sweetheart, or baby girl, either. It's Bella."

"Oh, you're going to be fun, aren't you?" His smile widens, his gray eyes lighting up.

I wriggle in his grip, trying to get him to let me go. He tugs me closer to his body instead.

"My name is Cormac," he rumbles, his voice like the purr of an engine. I like it far too much. "My friends call me Giant, but you'll call me Cormac."

"I think I'll go with Tiny," I mutter and then frown at him. "If you're as annoying as the other one, we're going to have problems, Tiny. I don't take orders, especially from strange men." My dad didn't raise me to be silent and follow along blindly. I'm opinionated, and I talk back.

Which is exactly how I ended up in this situation in the first place. But I'm not ready to think about that yet. If I do, I might cry. And I don't want to cry in front of this man. I'll do that when I'm alone later, and the pillow can soak up the evidence of my tears.

"I've got two rules, Mischief," Cormac says, completely ignoring me. "Don't put yourself in danger. And don't let another man put his hands on you. If you follow those rules, you and I are going to get along just fine. You break my rules, and I'll have you bent over my knee, pleading for mercy."

"You did not just say that," I gasp, shock running through me in a current.

"Said it. Meant it. Would say it again."

"So you're worse than the other one." An incredulous, hysterical laugh escapes before I can stop it. "Oh my God. This is not supposed to be my life. I don't even understand how this is my life right now. How is it that I witness a murder and end up a prisoner to a crazy giant while the men who did the crime run free?"

Cormac clamps a hand gently over my mouth. "Shh, Mischief," he says, his voice oddly soft. His expression matches. "You can rant and rave all you want when we get you home, but for now, we need you to be just another traveler. That's how we keep you safe."

I open my mouth to argue, and then Bellamy's lifeless eyes flash through my mind. The smell of blood bubbles to the surface of my memories, followed by the way the two shots echoed throughout the parking garage. They were so loud. So damn loud.

The desire to argue vanishes in a sickening lurch.

I drop my gaze with a defeated, weary nod.

Cormac carefully peels his hand away from my lips, leaving behind a tingle.

"Do you have any bags, Bella?"

I shake my head. "Just my backpack. Callum said I couldn't bring anything else."

"Safety precaution," Cormac says. "Checked bags can be tracked. We'll get you anything else you need once we get where we're going."

"And where is that, exactly?"

"No one told you?" His eyes widen.

"We were on a need-to-know basis," I say. "They didn't think I needed to know."

"Jesus Christ," he mutters. "No wonder you're pissed."

I stare at him levelly, not confirming nor denying his assessment. The truth is, I'm not angry anymore. I'm disappointed. My dad flipped his lid when the police showed up at his door to explain what happened. He's been in papa bear mode ever since. Not even my mom has been able to talk him down. I know he loves me, and he's only trying to keep me safe, but he's gone overboard this time. Way, way overboard.

And we both know he did it because he's worried that I'll do something to get myself hurt, not because he's afraid he can't protect me at home. He doesn't trust me to know my own limits. In his eyes, I'll always be the rash little girl who acts before she thinks. I'll never be an adult, not really. But I'm not telling that to a man I met five minutes ago, either.

Strangers know far too much about my family as it is, thanks to my biological mom, Marion. When my sister and

I were little, she went to prison for embezzling millions of dollars from my uncle and various other Fortune 500 companies. She tried to pin it on my dad because she hated that he loved us. We were big news in Tennessee for a long time because of it.

Growing up with the whole world knowing your mom tried to send your dad to prison because she hates you isn't easy. It's partly why my dad is so overprotective. Luckily, our stepmom, Jenna, is nothing like our biological mom. Jenna is a real mom. She loves me and my twin, Isla, un-conditionally. There's nothing she wouldn't do for us.

Marion was released from prison a few years ago. She still tries to keep in touch with us. Isla sees her every so often, but I said everything I needed to say to her a couple of years ago. She didn't want us when we were little. She tried to destroy our dad because he loved us. As far as I'm concerned, she isn't a mom to me. She's a stranger. I don't wish her any ill will, but I don't want to know her either.

"Here," Cormac says, hooking two fingers through the loop on my backpack. "Let me carry this for you, Mis-chief."

"I told you that's not my name, Tiny."

"Callum is former Special Forces. The man can track a goddamn terrorist through the desert with nothing but a ball of string and a speedo. You slipped out of his custody five minutes after you touched down," he rumbles, deftly stripping my backpack off my arms and out of my control.

His gray eyes meet mine, glinting with humor. "Believe me. You're nothing but mischief."

"A ball of string and a speedo?" I blink, not sure if he's kidding or not. Why did he need a speedo? No wonder Callum is so cranky, though. He's former military. He probably has better things to do than spend fifteen hours bouncing through every airport in the south. It still doesn't excuse him from staring at my ass.

Cormac winks, giving me another pirate's smile.

I get a little lost in his gaze.

He's way too handsome, and I'm way too tired to deal with that fact right now. Letting my guard down around this man is not a good idea. He'll bowl me right over and leave me wondering how it happened. I don't think I'd like being handled, not even by hands as sexy as his. And this man has man-in-charge written all over him. He's used to being in control and calling the shots. In his world, it's probably his way or the highway.

My stomach quivers at the thought of shaking up his world. I want to do it. I *want* to rattle him and throw his life entirely out of order just to see what he'll do. Will he really bend me over his knee like he threatened? Or is he a little bit wild too?

I have a feeling the answer to both is the same. He *would* spank me. He *is* wild.

Cormac "Giant" Carmichael is a conundrum.

That, I did not expect. Nor did I expect the little thrill that goes through me at the realization.

I rip my gaze from his, wrapping my arms around myself.

Do not let that pretty face soften you, I coach myself.

Except...I think he's already softening me.

"You brought your motorcycle?" I ask, coming to a dead stop when I see the monstrous chrome and red Harley pulled in beside a black truck in the long-term parking lot. It's a beast of a bike. Then again, Cormac is a beast of a man.

"Don't worry, Mischief." He shoots me a grin, flashing those dimples as he hefts my bag over his shoulder. "Callum is taking Beauty. We're taking his cage."

"Cage?" My brows furrow as I glance between him and Callum, who is two paces ahead.

He hasn't said a word since he caught up to us in baggage claim. I feel guilty for running off and ruining his night, but only a little. He did call me Satan's love child. And he was looking at my ass. Plus, he ate my plane snacks when I was in the bathroom on the last flight.

Stressing him out is the least he deserves for all of that. Besides, it's not like I was going to leave the airport without him. I may not be thrilled about my current situation, but I'm not a complete idiot either. The men who killed Bellamy are dangerous. I'm not going to go running all over Houston by myself and risk unraveling all the work we did to hide where I was going. I fully intended to wait for him in baggage claim. I just wanted to make him sweat a little first.

I didn't know he had reinforcements waiting.

"Truck." Cormac jerks his head at the truck. "Figured you'd prefer it over the bike."

"You're going to let Callum take your bike?" I eye him doubtfully. He named the bike. I don't think that means he's as blasé about letting someone else ride it as he seems.

Callum snorts as if he doesn't believe it either, confirming my suspicion. Cormac's only switching vehicles because of me. He thinks I'm too delicate to handle his manly man motorcycle. But my dad and uncle have been riding since Isla and I were babies. I loved riding with them when I was younger. I used to beg them to take me out. I drove them nuts, but nothing beats the feel of the wind in your face and the road beneath you.

"We can take the bike," I say, shrugging. "I just need a helmet."

Cormac cocks his head to the side. "You ride?"

"Since I was little." I give him a pointed look. "We'll get along a lot better if you don't assume that I'm afraid of everything because I'm not. Got it?"

A slow grin spreads across his face. "Fuck. I can't wait until you belong to me."

Callum nearly chokes on his tongue.

"I hope you don't mind waiting until hell freezes over," I say sweetly, patting Cormac on the chest as I sail past him. "Because I won't ever belong to you. I'm not property."

Cormac grabs my wrist, trapping it against his ridiculously hard chest. "Never said you were," he practically purrs, that sexy-as-sin voice washing over me. "I've never wanted to bend property over and eat it until it's screaming my name. You, on the other hand?" A possessive, predatory grow rumbles in his throat.

An inferno rages to life inside me, equal parts red-hot desire and white-hot offense. No one has ever spoken to me that way. I don't even think about it. I bring my knee up, aiming it directly at his groin.

For a giant, he's fast.

He sees the move before I even finish making it.

My knee connects with the inside of his thigh, narrowly avoiding the more sensitive parts I aimed for.

"Jesus Christ," Callum says and then barks laughter.

Somehow, I end up in Cormac's arms, my back to his chest.

"I'm going to let you get away with that one because I deserved it," he growls in my ear. "But next time you go for my balls, you better be ready for the consequences, Mischief."

"W-what consequences?" I ask, struggling to slip free of his grip. Except he's freaking He-Man, and there's no shaking him off. Good grief. What did his parents feed him? Trying to move him is like trying to move a brick wall. Only he doesn't feel like any wall I've ever felt. He's burning hot and curiously...safe.

God, I miss feeling safe. I miss Isla. I miss my bed and my life.

A surge of loneliness wells up from the pit of my stomach, sending tears into my eyes. I battle them back, refusing to cry.

"The one where you're seeing them up close and personal while I'm fucking my kid into you." His teeth close around the shell of my ear, delivering a stinging bite I feel all the way to my core. "Unless you're ready for that, I suggest you keep that sexy little attitude of yours leashed, little girl."

"I'm not a little girl," I growl.

"Believe me; I'm very fucking aware. My goddamn cock wouldn't be hard enough to pound steel if you were." His hot breath pelts my skin, his chest rumbling against my back. "But you're taunting a fucking lion here. The more you fight me, the more I want to settle your little ass down."

"That's because you're a crazy person."

"No, that's because we both know you're only fighting this hard because you're scared out of your mind and too damn stubborn to admit it. And I'm trying real fucking hard not to think about why you're so goddamn scared," he growls. "Because you need me here, not hopping a flight to Tennessee to handle the motherfuckers who hurt you. So I'm going to need you to take it down a notch so I can do my job without losing my mind. Otherwise, we're going to have bigger problems, and I'm thinking you've already got enough of those, baby."

"I am not scared," I whisper, my voice shaking.

"Yeah, you are. And that breaks my fucking heart." His arms tighten around me like he's hugging me. "You're safe now, Bella. So long as you're with me, you'll always be safe." His lips brush the shell of my ear. "Put it down for a little while, Mischief. I've got you now."

"Then stop saying I belong to you. You don't even know me."

"Oh, Mischief." He chuckles, the sound full of wicked intent as it ghosts along the side of my face, heating me to the nth degree. "I know you. I've been looking for you my entire life. I just didn't know it until I set eyes on you."

I'm not entirely sure what he means by that, but I'm not entirely sure he's wrong about it, either. For the first time in my life, something inside feels settled in a way it never has before, as if I've found something that's always been missing. A piece of me that I need. The feeling is terrifying. I don't want to need this man. I don't even want to like him.

I have plans for my life that don't include falling for a bossy giant. My future is in Tennessee, not in Texas. And yet...and yet this man makes it all too easy to see my path forward taking a different route. That's dangerous. *He's* dangerous.

I know what love can do to people. Look what it did to Marion. She destroyed herself, my dad, and my family for it. That won't ever be me. I'll never give anyone the power to turn me into what she became. And I think that weakness is in my blood. I've never even told Isla that, but it's true. My biggest fear is that I'm just like our bio-mom.

"Can we please just go already?" I sigh, keeping my gaze firmly on the ground to hide the tears blurring my field of vision. I want to burrow into Cormac's strength and let him keep it all afloat for a little while, but I can't do that. As soon as it's safe, I'm returning to my life. And he's staying here. It's better for him that way.

"Yeah," he says after a slight hesitation. "We can go, Mischief."

Chapter Three

Giant

I need to hire a priest. Shit. Do they even perform weddings if you aren't Catholic? I don't know, but it doesn't matter. I'll find someone willing to marry me and my girl. As soon as I convince her that she wants to marry me, anyway. The way I see it, I may need a week to talk her into it first. She's prickly.

Poor baby has been through hell. She's got the courage of a lion; I'll give her that. But I see the fear deep in those gorgeous baby blues. She's scared out of her mind and trying like hell not to show it. I don't think she wants me to know just how afraid she really is. My girl is strong and independent. She's a fierce little warrior.

I find that sexy as hell. I'm not made for a soft woman. I doubt one could handle me even if she tried. I've always had a little hellfire in my soul. Because of my job, I can be a bossy motherfucker. It comes with the territory. When you're responsible for keeping people alive, you gotta know your shit. I handle my business and know when to take things seriously. But if life isn't fun, what's the fucking point of living it? I drive my MC brothers up the fucking wall most of the time. They think I've got ADHD or some shit, but that's not it.

The truth is, I've just never felt settled. There's always been this vital piece of me missing. This *thing* that felt urgent, like I needed it now. It took me a long goddamn time to realize it wasn't a thing. It was a person. My soulmate. I've been missing her my entire life.

I'm not missing her now. I've finally found her. She's tucked up on the back of my bike, her arms wrapped tightly around my waist with her thighs cinched around me. I can feel the heat of her pussy against me. Feel her heart pounding against my back.

Bella Sterling is my missing piece.

And I'm mad as hell that someone tried to hurt her. That she watched someone die.

She's allowed to be as prickly as she wants. I won't ever hold it against her, not after what she's been through.

I've always wondered why I was built like a fucking brick shithouse. I'm guessing this is my answer. God or the universe or whoever is in charge knew I'd need to be massive to handle this fiery little goddess. They knew I'd need to be fearless to protect her. I'd need to be unwavering to win her trust. And I'd have to have the patience of a saint to keep my goddamn dick out of her. Because Je-*sus*. If he gets any harder, he's going to break off.

We pull up to the gate surrounding my property at a little after one in the morning. Callum idles on the road until we're through the gate and it's closed behind us, and then he takes off, heading to his place. The MC owns acres of undeveloped property on the south side of Cowboy's ranch. I picked the best damn piece of it and built my house right in the middle.

The two-story cabin is three miles into the woods. A deep gorge runs along the back of the property, cutting off access. It's the perfect place to protect clients in need of a place to fly under the radar for a little while. Unless you know the property well, you're more likely to land your ass in the gorge or on MC territory than to slip in or out undetected.

Motion lights flood the property with light as we start up the driveway, illuminating our way. Bella sits up a little straighter behind me, glancing all around, though there isn't much to see aside from trees and more trees. They end abruptly a half mile from the house in every direction. If anyone makes it onto the property, there is no place to hide for that last half mile. It's just them and a rolling expanse of green grass leading right up to the house.

I pull into the garage and park the bike before helping Bella dismount.

She stumbles, her legs unsteady after being in the same position for the entire ride from Houston. Shit. I should have stopped and let her stretch.

"Easy, Mischief," I murmur, sliding an arm around her waist to keep her on her feet.

"Thanks," she whispers.

I hang onto her for a moment, reluctant to let her go. She's cuddly as hell when she's not fighting me for every inch. A yawn cracks her jaws, her head drooping.

"Shit. Let's get you inside."

"Okay," she agrees softly.

I grab her backpack from my saddlebag and lead her toward the door.

Crash, the Rottweiler puppy Cash swindled me into adopting a few months ago, hears us coming. The crazy dog skids around the kitchen island like he's trying to win a race, his massive front paws extended to slow him down. There is no stopping him, though. The name picked the dog. He sails headfirst into Bella, knocking her back a step.

The bastard doesn't even look sorry about it.

He hops right up, his tongue lolling out as he stares up at her in complete adoration.

"Oh, my goodness," she whispers, dropping to her knees. "Aren't you the cutest?"

"He certainly thinks he is," I grumble, jealous as hell as she cups his face in her hands and coos at him. He eats it up, naturally. He may be a menace, but he's no fool. She's a goddess, and she's scratching his ears. Of course he's in heaven.

"What's your name, big guy?"

"This is Crash," I say, introducing them. "Crash, this is Mischief. She's going to be staying with us for a while, so I'm going to need you to act like you have at least two manners, my guy."

"Only two?" Bella turns to look up at me, an amused smile on her face. And goddamn, she's beautiful when she's happy. Callum wasn't lying when he said she was angelic. There isn't an angel in heaven any prettier than this sweet little thing.

"No licking his balls in front of you, and no farting," I say, ticking them off. "We're still working on the rest of it."

When I die, I want her laugh to be the last sound I hear. It goes straight to my fucking heart, setting off an avalanche. Entire sections get swept away, replaced with her. Fuck my life. How long do I have to wait to kiss her? To fuck her?

I've never been in a relationship. I haven't been on a date since my fucking senior prom. There have been plenty of opportunities, don't get me wrong. Women take one look at me and decide they want to know what it's like to fuck a man my size. But all it takes is one look at them for me to know they aren't who I've been looking for my whole life.

I should ask Fifth for guidance. He's the only one of my brothers who won't give me shit for not knowing the rules.

"How old is he?"

"Who?" I growl, eyes narrowed as white-hot jealousy courses through me. If she's thinking about Fifth, I will spank her.

"Crash?"

Oh, right.

She can't read your mind, idiot.

"Six months."

"He's so big."

He's not the only big thing around here, Mischief.

"He's a Rottweiler."

"I never would have guessed. I thought he was a Chihuahua."

I growl at her, which makes her laugh again.

And then she yawns.

"Are you hungry, Mischief?"

"Not really." A smile dances across her lips. "Callum bought me a sandwich on the plane."

Jealousy pings through me again. I may have to kill my cousin. It's unfortunate, really. He's my favorite cousin and a damn good business partner. Killing him will be all kinds of inconvenient for me. But it's inevitable at this point. He made my woman smile.

Her expression falls into an annoyed frown. "Of course, that was after he ate my plane snacks." Her gaze comes to me, her brows furrowed. "He reminds me of my little brother."

Ha! Yes. I don't have to kill my favorite cousin. He's in little brother territory. There's no leaving little brother territory once you enter it. Desire never even enters the fucking picture in little brother territory.

"Come on, Mischief." I hold out a hand to help her up. "Let's get you settled in so you can get some sleep."

She gives Crash another scratch and then allows me to pull her to her feet. Once she's steady, she immediately tries to remove her hand from mine. I link our fingers together instead, refusing to let her go. There's no time like the present for her to get used to me touching her. I plan to do a whole fucking lot of it.

She scowls at me and then mutters under her breath. I'm guessing it's not complimentary, so I choose to ignore it. My reality is far more pleasant than hers, anyway. In mine, she can't keep her hands off me. It's not a fantasy. It's just a future that we haven't quite caught up to yet. We're getting there, though. One step at a time.

I grab a bottle of water from the fridge and then lead her through the house, heading for the stairs with Crash following obediently behind. Bella gapes around her as if she's shocked that I don't live in a cave with pizza boxes spilling out of the damn trashcan or something. I don't. The furniture is modern and comfortable, and the art is expensive and tasteful. This house isn't a bachelor pad. It's a luxury safehouse designed to keep the rich, famous, and threatened nice and comfortable while they're in my care.

"Surprised?" I mutter to Bella.

"No," she lies.

I laugh quietly. "How much did your dad tell you about me, Mischief?"

"Not enough." The grumble in her voice makes my dick weep. "He didn't tell me that you live in a freaking fortress in the middle of the woods. Or that you're bigger than Goliath. And he definitely left out all the parts about you being bossy."

"This place isn't a fortress, but it's close," I admit. "If anyone comes looking for you, you'll be safe here. There are panic rooms on both floors of the house. The windows are bulletproof. I have security cameras and floodlights on the property, and my MC is located about two and a half miles away. The property is gated, and no one gets in or out unless I want them in or out."

"Okay," she whispers.

"I've been doing this a long time, baby. If I'm bossy, it's because I take your safety seriously. It's also because I know what you need, and I'm going to make sure you have it." I lead her up the stairs, stopping briefly at the top to point out which rooms are which. "You aren't a prisoner here, and I'm not a prison guard. This is your home now, and I'm the man willing to die to keep you alive."

"Because my dad is paying you," she mutters, her gaze sliding from mine. But not before I see the momentary flicker of emotion in them. Gratitude and distress chase one another through those baby blues as if she can't quite decide if she's grateful for my help or distressed at the thought of losing me.

I lead her down the hall to the primary bedroom. Anyone else would go in the guest suite, but I want her in my room. I want her head resting on my pillow and her curvy body wrapped in my sheets. When she sleeps, I want her surrounded by me, dreaming of me. I want my scent all over her, driving her fucking crazy every moment of the day.

"This is your room, Mischief," I murmur, pushing open the door for her.

Crash trots right in and hops up on the foot of the bed, making himself comfortable. I've never wanted to be a dog more. I'd fucking kill to be the one curling up in bed with her right now. But at least he'll be here to keep an eye on my girl until she's ready to let me in that bed with her.

"Is this your room?" she asks, eyeing me suspiciously.

"Nope," I lie, backing out of it before she calls me on my bullshit. "It's yours. The bathroom is on the left."

"No!" Bella cries, pure terror in her voice.

I fling my covers back and hit the floor running, my heart pounding as adrenaline rips through me. Crash whines from the primary bedroom as Bella cries out again. I damn near take the door to the guest room off the hinges as I burst out of it, trying to get to her.

I cross the hall in two steps, flinging open the door to her room.

My heart cracks in half as soon as I catch sight of her curled into a tiny ball in the middle of the bed, gripping my pillow so tightly her little fists are white. The blankets are twisted around her legs. Crash paces beside the bed, whining as if he doesn't know what to do. Every light in the room is on.

She's afraid of the dark. And having nightmares.

I close the door and kill the overhead lights, leaving the lamps on.

"Crash, settle," I whisper to the dog, pointing at the floor beside the bed.

He huffs at me and then reluctantly drops to his belly on the floor beside Bella.

I stalk to the bed, step around him, and gently lift Bella into my arms. "Easy, baby," I croon, holding her cradled against my chest. "I've got you."

"Cormac," she sighs. She doesn't open her eyes. I don't even think she wakes up, but she instantly settles, her body relaxing as the nightmare loses its hold on her and she steals every damn piece of my heart.

She's not sleeping alone tonight. Or any other night so long as nightmares plague her.

I crawl onto the bed, sitting with my back against the headboard and her in my arms. She sighs again, curling up against my chest with her head on my shoulder. Her brown ringlets cascade over my arm, wild and free. A pillow crease mars one perfect cheek.

I drag the blankets up over her, trying not to think about her hard nipples in that paper-thin t-shirt. Or about the fact that she's not wearing anything but a pair of panties underneath it. Now isn't the fucking time.

I close my eyes, breathing her in.

Her hand curls around my shoulder.

"Cormac," she sighs again.

"There's a giant in my bed," Bella whispers frantically. "Why is there a giant in my bed?"

I bite my lip, fighting a smile as she tries to carefully extricate herself from my arms without waking me up. It's far too late for that, though. I've been awake for an hour already. I probably should have gotten up and left her in peace, but she's cuddly as fuck. And I didn't want to be the asshole who sneaks into her bed in the middle of the night and then sneaks out of it without us having a conversation about it.

I'm pretty sure that rates high on the creepy meter.

"And he's half naked." She whimpers, turning my cock to steel. "I'm half naked. Oh my god. We're half-naked in bed together, and I'm wearing Snoopy underwear."

"I've never been more jealous of a fucking dog in my entire goddamn life, Mischief," I growl, wrapping one arm around her and rolling her beneath me. "Never wanted to kiss one more than I do right now either." That little fucker is all that's standing between me and her sweet cunt.

"Cormac!" she shouts, her blue eyes comically wide. A pink blush creeps across her cheeks. "You're in my bed."

"Actually, you're in mine."

"I knew you were a liar!" she cries.

Fuck, it's too early for her to be this beautiful.

"You can't just lie to get what you want, you know. That's not how the real-world works. And what do you think you're doing in bed with–?"

I dip my head, covering her mouth with mine. I can't help it. She's reading me the riot act, looking all rumpled and sexy, and I need to know what she tastes like right *now*.

Her breath leaves her lungs in a rush as she falls silent. Her hands fly to my shoulders. I half expect her to push me away and try to kick my ass...but she doesn't. She freezes with her hands on my shoulders for a split second, and then she whines and tries to pull me closer.

Ah, goddamn.

I grunt, flicking my tongue out to get a taste of her. Just one. At least, that's what I tell myself. Even as I say it, I know damn well that I'm lying. One taste won't ever be enough, not when it comes to her. I've been starving for her my entire life. I plan to drown myself in her to quench my thirst.

She tips her head back, eagerly opening to me as I lick inside her mouth, taking more like the greedy motherfucker I am. My hand runs down her side, dragging her leg up over my hip. As soon as I feel her hot cunt against the hard ridge of my erection, I growl and rip my mouth away from hers, breathing hard.

She presses her fingers to her lips, staring up at me in wide-eyed shock. "You can't do that."

"Yeah? I just did."

"Don't do it again." There's no heat in the demand, no power. She says it by rote, as if she's only saying it because it's what she's supposed to say. We both know she doesn't mean it. I see that truth glittering in her eyes.

"Why not?"

"I didn't like it."

"Liar." I nudge her hand away from her mouth to run my thumb along her bottom lip. "You loved it. We both know you did, Mischief. I've got the nail imprints on my shoulders and the wet spot on my boxers to prove it."

She doesn't say anything for a long moment. She simply stares at me. I think she's trying to see into my soul, to read my intentions. Whatever she finds there doesn't seem to reassure her. If anything, it seems to distress her. Worry fills her expression.

"Don't make me fall for you, Cormac," she finally whispers, her voice shaking.

"There will be no falling involved, Mischief," I say, pressing a gentle kiss to her forehead. "I intend to hold you the whole fucking way down."

CHAPTER FOUR

Bella

"How often are you having nightmares?" Cormac asks, eyeing me over the marble island.

I swallow my toast, not sure I'm ready to answer this question. But I can tell by the look in his eyes that he already knows I'm having them frequently. Is that why he was in my bed last night? It wasn't why he kissed me this morning. It's definitely not why I kissed him back.

I didn't mean to do it, but I couldn't stop myself, either. He's dangerous to my self-control. Actually, he's dangerous to virtually every part of me. Staying vigilant and guarding my heart around him is going to be impossible when he insists on slipping beneath my defenses before I even realize he's moved.

"Too often," I mutter, dropping the toast to my plate.

"How often, Bella?"

"Every night."

He grunts, clearly not thrilled with that answer.

"Sorry if I woke you up last night."

He sets his coffee mug on the counter, circling around the island to me. One thick finger settles beneath my chin, gently tilting my face up to his. "You don't owe me an apology for how you deal with trauma," he says. Early morning sunlight spills across his face, lighting him in a nimbus of soft white. "You don't owe *anyone* an apology."

Who *is* this man?

Your future, a little voice whispers.

I'm not sure what scares me more. The possibility that it's right, or the fact that I hate the thought less and less every time I have it. Cormac Carmichael is magnetic, and I'm slowly being pulled closer and closer to his field. Pretty soon, there will be no escaping it.

"I keep dreaming about what happened," I whisper, my stomach twisting into knots. "Um, the therapist said it's pretty common after something like that."

Cormac nods, his expression soft. "Are you taking anything to help you sleep?"

I quickly shake my head. "It just made the nightmares worse."

He feathers his fingers along my jaw, flashing those deadly dimples at me. "Guess that means you'll just have to get used to sharing my bed then, Mischief."

"Yeah, with Crash."

"Nah, with me." His dimples deepen, his thumb brushing across my bottom lip. Little flames of desire spread throughout me, licking at my skin, and then sinking deep to pool in my belly. My nipples harden, and every bit of moisture disappears from my mouth. "You didn't have a nightmare when you were in my arms."

"Probably because you're a giant," I mumble, my gaze riveted to his mouth. That wicked, perfect mouth. I want him to kiss me again. I *need* him to kiss me again. Just one more taste. Just one more, and then I can go back to thinking rationally.

"You were saying my name in your sleep."

"Cormac."

"Yeah, just like that," he growls.

I don't know what possesses me to do it, but I say it again. "Cormac."

"You're going to get yourself in trouble, little girl."

"I told you already, my name is Bella, *Tiny*."

"You just can't help yourself, can you, Mischief?"

"No." I meet his gaze, challenging and bold, as defiant as ever. "I told you I don't follow orders. I'm not obedient. I've never been a good girl, Cormac."

He slips his hand around to the back of my head, spearing his fingers through my hair. I groan as he grips the strands tightly, craning my head back until I'm practically prostrate on the island beneath him, those gray eyes locked on mine.

"Defy me," he growls. "Fight me. Torture me, Mischief. Make me work like a fucking dog to please you. But don't *ever* think you aren't perfect exactly the way you are. I'm not interested in obedience. I'm interested in *you*. And you've had my heart beating out of my damn chest since I set eyes on you."

I stare up at him, my heart pounding so loud I'm sure he can hear it. I certainly can. It thumps against my ribcage in rattling strikes, shaking me to my core. *He's* shaking me to my core. And I don't even know where to begin processing that.

I need my sister. She always knows what to do. But she isn't here now, is she? Isla can't help me solve this giant problem. This time, it's up to me to figure it out on my own.

Cormac leans down, brushing his lips against mine in a soft pass.

Before I can even react, he peels himself off me and steps back.

"Get ready to go, Mischief. We're leaving in twenty."

I drag myself upright to see him striding from the kitchen, the muscles in his back flexing. "Where are we going?" I shout after him.

"To see my brothers!" he shouts back.

Twenty-five minutes later, we pull up outside of a ranch. At least, it looks like a ranch. The row of motorcycles pulled up out front leads me to believe it's not your typical ranch. So does the Silver Spoon MC logo emblazoned across the entrance to the property.

"You're in an MC," I say once Cormac helps me off his bike, not sure how I forgot that tidbit. My dad mentioned it. Cormac did too when he was telling me about the property yesterday.

"I am," he rumbles, removing my helmet. His gray eyes meet mine, probing and curious. "Does that bother you, baby?"

I eye him levelly. "You live in a fortress in the woods," I say. "You own a multi-million dollar company that does security for rockstars and foreign dignitaries. My dad trusts you with me, and he doesn't trust anyone with me and my sisters. No, it doesn't bother me."

He rewards me with those dimples and another pirate smile, making my knees weak. My pulse races, electricity crackling in the air between us as if it's alive.

He leans in, his gaze dropping to my lips.

He's going to kiss me again.

My stomach bottoms out. I sway toward him, eager to feel his lips on mine again. To feel his heat engulfing me again. I ache for it.

God help me; every part of me aches to feel this man all over me.

"Get your big ass in here, Giant!" a deep voice booms from the front porch of the ranch, amusement lacing his tone.

"Tick tock, motherfucker," someone else shouts.

"I hate every single one of you motherfuckers," Cormac says conversationally, lifting his middle finger into the air.

Loud laughter spills across the yard to us.

"I think your brothers know we're here," I whisper, feeling the burn in my cheeks. They almost caught us kissing. God only know what they think. Oddly...I don't care. Let them think it.

"Sucks for me," Cormac growls, still hyperfocused on my mouth. "Because I'm starving for another taste of you, Bella."

My tongue slips out, sliding across my bottom lip.

Cormac growls again, the dark, predatory sound coming from deep in his chest. Chills erupt all over my body, and my core clenches.

Oh, my goodness.

Abort, Bella. Abort right now.

Except I can't. Except I don't want to. I'm caught in his spell, tangled like prey in a sticky web. And every minute I spend in it only pulls me in deeper.

Cormac exhales a breath and then takes a step back, twisting to set my helmet on the back of his bike. I suck in a lungful of fresh air, trying to clear my head. It's a useless attempt. *His* scent still lingers, making me dizzy.

"Come on. Let's go meet these assholes," he mutters, turning back to me. He grabs my hand, lacing our fingers together.

For the first time, I turn to face the group on the porch. And whoa. Cormac's MC is not like any MC I've ever heard of before now. They're all hot, for one. They're an implacable wall of muscle lining the front porch, each of them gorgeous, each of them wearing an amused grin. Half of them wear suits. The others are dressed more casually, with cuts stretched across their chests. But it's evident they're all as wealthy as Cormac.

They all eye me with various degrees of curiosity as we approach. None seems annoyed by my presence here, though. If anything, they seem...amused. Relieved. The one on the end who looks like he stepped out of a fashion magazine seems genuinely happy as he glances between me and Cormac.

"Fuckers, this is Mischief. You assholes call her Bella. Bella, these fuckers *were* my MC brothers until three minutes ago," Cormac says by way of introduction.

"We're still your brothers, motherfucker."

"Maybe," Cormac grunts. "I've decided I don't like any of you that much."

"Don't be rude to your brothers, Cormac."

"Yeah, Cormac," the first one who spoke— a handsome dark-haired man with green eyes— says, smirking. "Don't be rude to your brothers."

Cormac flips him off and then turns to me. "Mischief, this is Jason Montoya. We call him Cash. He's our prez, though I couldn't tell you why."

"Someone has to keep your big ass in line," Cash— the man so just spoke— mutters and then winks at me. "It's nice to meet you, sweetheart. "Sorry you've been saddled with this asshole."

"Doesn't look like she minds too much from where I'm standing," a man in a cowboy hat drawls, smiling at me.

My cheeks heat.

"Blink twice if you're in need of rescue," he says.

"I will kill you," Cormac says without heat, pulling me back a step.

His brothers all laugh. The cowboy's smile grows.

"This is Landon. We call him Cowboy. You'll never guess why." Cormac rolls his eyes, but I see the humor in them. He's only teasing. He points at the man in glasses next, the one covered in tattoos. "This is Finn, also known as Hacker."

"You're a hacker?" I ask, impressed. He doesn't look like any computer nerd I've ever met.

"He's a fucking genius," Cormac answers for him. "Don't let that fool you though, Mischief. He's still an idiot."

"Man, fuck you," Hacker says, laughing.

"This is Rafe. We call him Lynch."

I eye the man standing next to Hacker, a little afraid to ask how he got his nickname.

"Grew up in Lynchburg," he says as if reading my mind.

"I'm Tate. They call me Hands," the guy next to Lynch says, smiling at me.

"He's a pediatric surgeon."

"Don't forget pain in the ass," Cash supplies.

"Right." Cormac grins at me. "He's a pain-in-the-ass pediatric surgeon."

"And then we've got Bender." Cormac points to him, but I recognize him. It's hard not to know who he is when his band was one of the biggest in the world. "Jude, Fifth." The man in the fancy suit beside Bender gives me a smile. "Prince Damien De Angelis. We call him Angel. I don't know why. He's the fucking devil."

Angel laughs, flipping him the bird. "It's nice to meet you, Bella."

"Um, you too," I whisper, not exactly sure how I'm supposed greet a prince. But I figure if he's flipping Cormac off, I can probably skip a curtsey.

"And this," Cormac says, turning me gently to face the man on the end, "is Andreas Romano, Playboy."

I can tell by the way he introduces him that Andreas is special to him, his closest friend. It's obvious Andreas feels the same way about Cormac. The bond between them is apparent.

"Hi, Andreas."

"It's good to finally meet you, Bella," he says as if he's been waiting a long time. He meets Cormac's gaze over my head. "Changed your mind about the water, didn't you?"

"Fuck off," Cormac mutters, making Andreas smile.

"Another one bites the dust," Tate says and then laughs. "Jesus. The girls are going to love this."

"Speaking of the girls," Cormac says. "Mischief needs clothes, shoes, makeup, shampoo, all the girly shit. Help a brother out?"

"You want the girls to take her shopping?" Cash asks.

Cormac shakes his head. "I need the shopping to come to her." He releases me long enough to pull his wallet out of his pocket and hand over a credit card.

"Shit." Cash grins, taking possession of the card. "I'll gladly let our wives go on a spree with your money. Consider it payback for all the shit you've given us for the last year and a half. Just don't say I didn't fucking warn you when they buy out the entire goddamn mall."

"I don't need that much," I protest, feeling guilty. I brought a couple of outfits with me. With a few more, I'll be fine. "Just a few things."

"It's fine, Mischief," Cormac says, running a hand down my arm. "I can afford it. Besides, you're worth whatever damage they do."

An hour later, Rafe, Cowboy, and Tate leave with half of the wives for the mall. The others stay behind to help Rulie and Gloria, the older couple who are like parents to the MC, take care of the babies. There are a lot of them! My head is spinning a little bit.

I never realized just how much like family an MC could be, but this one is. Even their clubhouse is like one giant house where they all spend time together with their families. It's organized chaos.

There's so much love between everyone. Seeing them together makes me homesick in a way I've never been before now. I've always been just a short drive from home, able to visit at any time. Isla and I have never gone more than a few hours without speaking. But I'm not even allowed to call or text her in case anyone is tracking me.

I miss my twin intensely. She's always been the one constant in my life, with me even in the womb. What's she doing right now? Is she missing me too?

"We need to talk, Bella," Cormac murmurs as he, Cash, Fifth, Hacker, Bender, Angel, and Andreas all file into the living room, grim-faced and unsmiling. Samara, Tate's wife, follows behind. I think Cormac asked her to stay so I wouldn't feel outnumbered and overwhelmed. I liked her immensely. All of the wives are really sweet. I'm really looking forward to getting to know them.

Samara and Cormac immediately cross to me. Cormac picks me up from the couch before sitting down with me in his lap. Samara takes a seat beside us.

I don't bother arguing with Cormac about putting me in his lap. I can tell by the expression on his face what his brothers want to talk about, and I can use a little of his strength. My stomach trembles, anxiety quaking through me.

Samara gives me a sympathetic smile, making me intensely grateful she's here. I like her. There's a quiet strength to her, an unyielding spirit that I recognize. She's known darkness in her life.

Cormac's brothers settle in around the room, each taking seats instead of hovering or looming. Once they're all situated, Fifth leans forward, his hands steepled together.

He's an interesting man.

"We need to ask you about Bellamy Hill, sweetheart," he says, his deep voice quiet and grave. "I understand it's probably not something you want to think about, much less discuss, but in order for us to protect you to the best of our abilities, we need to know what we're up against here."

"I thought Cormac was protecting me," I mutter, stalling. He's right. I don't want to talk about it.

"We don't fight alone in this brotherhood," Cash says. "What one of us endures, we all endure. You're under our protection now, Bella."

Of course. They're family.

"Talk to me, baby," Cormac says. "Tell me what happened."

I expel a breath. "There isn't a lot to tell. Bellamy was working late like always. I had some things to finish up, so I stayed over. When I was done, he asked if I could do him a favor before I left and run something down to the studio, so they'd have it in the morning," I say. "He went to the parking garage, and I went to drop off the flash drive. The studio is only one floor from the garage, so I decided to take the stairs."

Cormac runs soothing hands up and down my arms.

"I heard arguing when I made it to the garage. Two men had Bellamy pinned to the ground, demanding money from him. They kept saying he owed them." I shiver at the memory. Bellamy kept shouting that he'd get them whatever they wanted, but they didn't want to hear it.

They were so violent.

"I just...froze. I didn't know Bellamy had a panic button on his keyfob. Neither did they. One of them stomped on his hand, and he let go of his keys. That's when they realized he'd been pressing the button. Um, they got mad." I flinch, cowering into Cormac.

"The younger of the two kicked him in the stomach. The older one pulled out a gun and shot him twice." I cower deeper into Cormac, grateful when Samara reaches for my hand, gripping it tightly. "I screamed."

"Jesus," Cash whispers.

Cormac growls, a low, menacing sound.

"I didn't mean to do it."

"I'm so damn sorry, Bella," Cash says, his expression rife with remorse. "You never should have had to see that."

"They heard me," I whisper, licking my lips. "The youngest started coming toward me. I turned and ran back inside the building. Um, you have to have the code to get in, and they didn't have the code. A few minutes later, they peeled out of the parking deck in a black Charger." I exhale a shaky breath. "I waited for a minute to make sure they were gone, and then I tried to help Bellamy until the police got there."

He was already beyond help, but I tried anyway. I couldn't just leave him. The whole time, I was terrified they were going to come back and kill me too. But Bellamy was a friend. He took a chance on me when no one else would. I couldn't leave him to die alone.

"They must have gotten a good look at me," I mumble. "Two days later, someone set my car on fire. The next day, they broke into my apartment and trashed it."

"Do the police have any leads?"

"The Dixie Mafia."

"Motherfucker," Cormac curses, tension radiating from him.

Cash and Andreas look shell-shocked. Fifth just looks worried.

"Um, they think Bellamy owed them drug money. I don't think it was Bellamy though. I think it's his son, Brantley. Um, the musician." I meet Fifth's gaze. "I had access to Bellamy's bank account. Drug addicts aren't as careful with money as he was."

Fifth gives me a barely perceptible nod.

"Brantley looks like he has it all together, but he doesn't. I heard him and Bellamy arguing about something Bellamy was worried people were going to find out about. If he owed drug money, they'd go after Bellamy."

"She's not wrong," Bender says. "If you can't squeeze blood from a turnip, you move to the thing you can squeeze it from."

No one disagrees with him. They can't. Criminals target family members all the time. There is no honor amongst thieves and monsters. If there were, I wouldn't be here now. Bellamy wouldn't be dead now.

"The Dixie Mafia," Andreas muses out loud.

"They aren't getting their fucking hands on her," Cormac swears, steely resolve in his voice. "I don't care if we have to kill every single one of the motherfuckers to get that point across. Bella is off-limits."

"Agreed," Andreas says.

"Agreed," the rest of the brothers echo.

Chapter Five

Giant

"Cash tried to warn you," Bella says, biting her bottom lip to hide that fucking perfect smile. "You didn't listen."

I grunt, staring at the eight thousand bags of shit my brothers just dropped off in my living room. It looks like the goddamn mall exploded in here. "Every woman in this town is going to be knocking on my door, asking to borrow bras and shit."

Bella gives up trying to fight her amusement and devolves into a fit of laughter. "Oh, Tiny," she says, wiping her eyes. "You have so much to learn."

"Yeah?" I cock a brow at her. "You going to teach me, Mischief?"

She meets my gaze, her baby blues far lighter than they were when we left the clubhouse an hour ago. Talking about what she saw wasn't easy for her. Hearing it wasn't easy for me. I've never been as certain of two things simultaneously as I am of these: Bella Sterling is utterly goddamn fearless, and I'm never letting her out of my sight.

My poor, brave girl. I've known men twice her age and three times her size who wouldn't do what she did—go back to help a man down. She did it. Even scared out of her mind and completely alone, she did it. I wanted to fucking howl when she told us that. It's no wonder she's having nightmares. She didn't just watch her friend die. She tried to save his life while he bled out in a goddamn parking garage, and she did it by herself, unsure if the motherfuckers who shot him would come back to kill her too.

She's not just fearless. She's a warrior. If Valhalla is real, she's earned her place there.

"Maybe," she whispers. And then she swallows hard. "But I want something, Cormac."

"Name it."

"I want to talk to my family." Her expression sobers, a shadow drifting across her angelic face. "And before you tell me it's not safe or that it's not allowed, I already know all of that. My dad told me before he took my cell phone. But you have a genius hacker in your MC. Surely between the two of you, you can figure out a way for me to talk to them safely."

Shit. I should have told her already.

"Come here, Mischief." I hold my hand out and wait for her to come to me. As soon as she places her hand in mine, I pull her into my arms, dragging her up against my chest where she belongs. "I talked to your dad briefly last night while you were in the shower," I murmur into her hair. "He knows you're here and that you're safe."

They're no closer to catching the fuckers than they were when she left. Nashville PD is chasing leads, but they don't have anything solid yet. No names, no identities, nothing but the descriptions Bella provided and a vehicle with a stolen license plate.

Her shoulders slump, some of the tension draining from her body.

"And I've already got Hacker working on getting us a secure connection so you can talk to your mom and your sisters whenever you want," I promise. "Figured you'd be missing home and want to talk to your family."

"I miss my twin," she whispers, her voice a mere scrap of sound.

The sorrow in her voice breaks my goddamn heart. "I'll fix it, baby."

"She's mad at me." Her eyes meet mine, wide and watery. That breaks my heart too. She hasn't cried since she got here, but she's crying because her sister's mad at her. This little goddess may act tough, but underneath, she's as soft as they come. "She gets mad when she's worried."

I brush her tears away with the pads of my thumbs. "Then it's a damn good thing you've got me and Crash looking out for you now, isn't it?" I murmur, sliding my hand around to cup the back of her head. I press my lips to her forehead and then to her cheeks, kissing away her tears. "Because we aren't going to let anything happen to you. You're safe with us, and she's got nothing to worry about anymore."

Hell will freeze over before I allow anyone to harm this girl. She's mine. No one will get close to her. No one will touch her. I've protected rockstars and royalty and every-one in between, and I've never failed. She will be safe. Not because I'm good at what I do but because it matters more this time. It's personal now.

She crept into my chest and stole my heart like a thief in the night. It beats for her now. My whole damn world is re-ordering itself with her securely at the center. It's the most natural feeling in the world, too. There's nothing strange about it, nothing jolting or disorienting. It feels...damn good. Like I've been living with half a soul for thirty-five years and finally learned how to breathe.

I scoop her up into my arms and carry her upstairs to the bedroom. Crash lifts his head from the couch to look at us and then huffs and lays back down. I think he's pissed that we ran off and left him at home this morning.

"What are you doing?" Bella watches me through wide, dilated eyes when I lay her out on the bed and then pull her shoes off. Her little toes are painted purple. Somehow, even her feet are sexy to me. I bring each one to my mouth, kissing her instep before I replace it on the bed.

"We're taking a nap."

"Oh." Her eyes darken when I yank my shirt off over my head. Her greedy gaze prowls across my torso, eating up the sight of me. And goddamn, if that doesn't make me feel fifty feet tall and bulletproof. My girl likes what she's seeing. It's a good thing because I plan to be the only man she sees like this.

I know damn well that I should leave my pants on, but she isn't the only one who doesn't follow instructions and doesn't obey orders. She isn't a good girl, and I'm damn sure not a good man. I was born with hellfire in my soul. I tempt fate and taunt the devil just because I fucking can. So I strip down to my boxers, growling when her gaze shifts down my body, focusing on my cock.

"Look your fill, little girl," I rumble, gripping my shaft through the fabric. I squeeze the greedy beast, letting her get a good look at what she'll be getting just as soon as she's on the same page as me. "You made him this way."

"Jesus, Cormac," she whispers. "I think I need to stop calling you Tiny."

"Don't."

Her gaze flits back to mine.

"I like it," I say with a shrug. "Mischief and Tiny."

She smiles, a blinding smile that damn near knocks me on my ass. Jesus Christ, I can't wait until she falls in love with me too. I'm going to follow her around like a lovesick puppy.

"Your turn, Mischief. Strip."

I expect her to tell me to go to hell. Bella doesn't do anything she doesn't want to do. But she doesn't tell me that. Instead, she sits upright, reaching for the hem of her shirt. It's only after she yanks it off over her head that I realize she isn't wearing a bra.

"Your tits are out," I growl.

"You told me to strip."

"You aren't wearing a bra."

She eyes me oddly.

"Lose the pants, Mischief." If she doesn't have panties covering my pussy, I'm spanking it. And then I'm eating it. She'll just have to be mad about it after she comes on my tongue. Because those sexy leggings are too goddamn tight for her to be around my brothers with no panties.

She lifts her hips, shimmying out of her pants.

Snoopy peeps at me from between her thighs.

Part of me snarls in rage. The other part sighs in relief.

I run my gaze all over her, memorizing every curvy inch of her body. Bella isn't a small girl. She isn't reed thin. She's the perfect pear shape, exactly the kind of woman a man like me could get lost in. There's enough of her to grip onto, enough of her to cushion me while I'm driving into that little slice of heaven between her legs.

"Damn," I breathe, squeezing my cock. "I knew you were beautiful, but *goddamn*, baby."

She presses her thighs together, her cheeks flushing with heat. "Thanks, I think."

"As soon as you're in love with me, I'm going to feast on that perfect body," I growl. "Every goddamn inch of it will know what I feel like all over it, Bella."

"Cormac," she whispers, her voice shaking on my name. "I'm *not* falling in love with you."

I'm not sure if she's trying to convince me or herself. Neither of us is buying what she's selling.

"I already told you, Mischief," I murmur, sliding into the bed with her. I grab her around the waist, hauling her up against me. My dick settles between her cheeks like he's nestling into his home. "I plan to hold you the whole way down."

She whimpers, a sexy little sound that does a number on my cock.

I press my lips to her shoulder and then pull the covers up over us.

We lay quietly for several heartbeats and then Bella moans my name, pushing her ass back against me. She doesn't say a word, but I know exactly what she's after, exactly what she wants. My girl needs to come.

"Say it, Mischief," I growl, splaying my hand across her belly.

"Please."

"Give me the words, baby. I'll give you exactly what you want, but not until you give me permission to put my hands right where you want them."

"Cormac, please," she whispers."

"Say it."

She sobs my name, frustration and need mingling in her voice. Her legs move restlessly on the bed, shifting against mine as she tries to get comfortable. She can't, though. She needs to come too badly. But Bella is a stubborn, fiery little goddess determined to make me crazy. I tried a million times to envision the woman I'd end up with, but I never saw this one coming. In a million years, I never would have seen the female version of me coming for me like a freight train. Perhaps my big ass should have been prepared for the impact, but I wasn't.

I'm not prepared for her next move either.

She doesn't give me the words. She slips her hand down her stomach, her fingers trailing across mine as they quest downward. My breath gets caught in my throat as she moves lower, slipping that little hand into her panties. Cum shoots from my shaft, landing hot and sticky against my boxers as the sounds of Mischief touching her pussy reach my ears.

She's so wet. So damn wet.

"Cormac," she moans, writhing against my chest as her fingers slip through her soaked folds.

I growl her name, my self-control torn in two. I drag my hand down her belly, feeling the way her muscles quiver beneath my palm, and then shove my hand into her panties with hers. "Do it," I snarl in her ear. "Fuck yourself with your fingers while you're crying out my name, Mischief."

I drag the back of her panties down with my other hand, and then free my cock.

She jolts when she feels my erection against her cheeks. And then ruins me for anyone else when she immediately presses back against me, curious and eager.

"Lift your leg," I demand, tapping her hip.

For once, she obeys me. She lifts her leg, allowing me to slide my cock between her legs from behind. I nearly choke on my own damn tongue when I feel her hot cunt kissing the tip. Goddamn, she's soaked. Hot. *Heaven.*

"Now make yourself come," I growl, pumping my hips so my dick slides through her folds. I don't try to enter her. I'm not stupid enough to think she's ready for that yet. But that doesn't mean I can't give her a little taste of what it'll be like between us when she is mine.

We work together, strumming her clit as I lick and suck at her neck and jerk myself off between her messy thighs. My dick nudges at her little fuckhole. I torture us both, letting it rest there, rubbing it against her. I dip the tip in, just the tip.

"Ah, Christ. Jesus, Mischief." I bury my face in her hair, trying not to come unglued when she pushes back, trying to take more of me. "Behave before I have you pinned face down fucking my kid into you while you're screaming the roof down around us."

"Already told you," she gasps, her fingers flying across her hard little clit. "I d-don't behave."

"Too bad." I bite the side of her neck, pulling the skin between my teeth. "I don't fuck on the first nap, little girl. Now, fucking come before I spank your pretty little ass for fucking with me."

"M-make me."

Oh, I can't wait until she's mine. I'm going to have so much fun teaching her exactly what she needs to settle her little ass down. She'll fight me for every inch, making me prove that I deserve her submission. And I'll work her over while earning it. Every fucking day with her will be a revelation.

"Get that perfect hand out of my way and on my cock," I growl, batting hers aside.

She reaches for my dick, leaving me writhing in sweet torment when her fingers close around me. Ah, Jesus. She needs to come now because I'm about to lose it all over her perfect cunt. Her hand is slippery with her juices as she tries to work it up and down the few inches of my shaft that she can reach.

I work around her hand, pressing my thumb to her hard clit.

Her hips lift from the bed, a startled cry breaking from her lips. She makes the same sound when I press one thick finger inside her tight little hole. Jesus, she's a vise around me, squeezing the fuck out of my finger. I work it in and out of her, teasing her hole while I strum her clit with my thumb.

"It'll feel even better when it's my cock, Mischief," I whisper against her ear. "You'll feel like I'm going to split you in two, but you won't ever want it to end. You'll plead with me not to stop. You'll ache for more." My teeth close around the shell of her ear, delivering a small bite.

She sobs my name, her body trembling against mine.

"You'll feel me every time you move, Bella," I breathe, soothing the bite with my tongue. "And you'll beg for more." I curl my finger up to stroke her g-spot. "I'll be your own personal heaven, little girl. You'll live and breathe for me."

"Cormac!" she shouts, coming unglued at the seams. Her cunt grips my finger, fluttering as she unravels around me. She trembles, a sexy moan rippling through the room.

Watching her come—hearing her moaning my name—sends me over the edge with her. I bury my face in her neck, groaning as my balls draw up and cum spills from my shaft, soaking her hand and her thighs. I pump my hips, covering her thighs and pussy in my seed.

"Fuck, fuck," I gasp, trying to breathe through the rush of pure damn ecstasy coursing through me. I pull her close, nuzzling my face against her neck. "Goddamn, Mischief." And then, because I can't help myself, I scoop a little bit of cum from her thigh with my thumb, pushing it inside her where it should be. Where it will be from now on.

"What are you doing?" she asks.

"Putting this where it belongs." I push it in deep and then rub the rest of it into her skin. She moans quietly, making me smile. She might not know it yet, but she's already falling for me. If she weren't, she'd be kicking my ass right now. "Now you smell like me."

"Shut up and go to sleep, Tiny," she says in response.

I laugh quietly.

Fuck, she's incredible.

When I wake up, shadows cling to the corners of the room, and I'm in bed alone. Mischief is nowhere to be found. I quickly throw on a pair of pants and head downstairs to find her, not thrilled she managed to sneak out of the bed without me knowing. I want to know every move she makes.

"Mischief?" I shout, jogging down the stairs.

The house is quiet...too quiet.

The hair on the back of my neck stands up.

"Crash," I call, snapping my fingers.

He doesn't come running, either.

The lamp in the living room is on. All of Mischief's shit is still piled in a heap by the door where my brothers left it. I quickly make a circuit through the house, checking every room. There's a glass of water sitting on the island, and she fed Crash, but neither of them is anywhere to be found.

Fuck.

Where are they?

Icicles form around my heart, worry kicking in. If she tried to run off, Crash would follow her. He's in love with her too. She doesn't know the property, though. She doesn't know about the gorge. It's getting dark. She could miss it and fall in. She could get lost. Someone could snatch her up and disappear with her.

How long has she been gone?

"Fuck!" I shout, panic setting in.

I run back into the living room to grab my phone and shoes, afraid for the first time in my life. I just found her. I can't lose her now. I won't fucking survive it. Already, she's the most important thing in my life. She's the reason for all of this, the thing I've been working toward for as long as I can remember. I've always been preparing for her, trying to ensure I was ready to take care of her.

If I've already failed.... No, that's not possible.

I grab my phone and dial Cash's number, trying to shove my feet into my shoes at the same time.

"Yo," he says.

"She's missing."

"What the fuck?"

"She's missing, and I need to find her. I have to find her," I ramble. "Send everyone."

"Calm down, Giant," Cash says, his voice firm. "Tell me what happened."

"I just goddamn told you," I growl. "She's missing, and I need..."

The front door opens.

Crash comes bounding inside, fucking up the rug in front of the door. Bella's hot on his heels, her ringlets all wild around her laughing face, her eyes bright with humor. My stomach bottoms out, relief hitting me like a fist.

"Never mind," I growl to Cash. "I found her."

"What the fu–?"

I hang up on him.

Crash makes a beeline for the couch, running right through the pile of bags.

"Crash!" Bella cries as they scatter every which way. "You wicked dog."

I drop my phone to the coffee table, storming across the room toward her.

"Hi, sleepyhead," she says, smiling up at me.

"You left the house without permission," I growl.

Her smile slips, uncertainty drifting through her expression. "I took Crash outside."

"You left the house without permission," I say again. Part of me wants to yank her into my arms and kiss the shit out of her. The other part wants to bend her over and spank her ass for scaring me. Right now, I'm not sure which side is winning the war. My life just flashed before my damn eyes. I saw her laying at the bottom of that gorge. I saw someone driving off with her in the trunk. It's fucking me up.

"I didn't know I needed permission to take the dog outside, Cormac," she says, her chin coming up. "You were sleeping, and he was restless. I thought he could use a little exercise. Frankly, I needed a little fresh air too."

"You tell me when you leave this house, Bella."

"You were asleep!"

"Then you wake me up! You don't leave this house without permission!" I roar.

She rears back in shock, her face paling.

Shit.

"Yes, sir," she says, her tone clipped.

I reach for her to apologize for yelling, but she slips around me, her back ramrod straight. She bends to scoop up an armload of bags from the floor.

"Bella."

"I'm going to go put these away," she says.

"Bella."

"And then I'm going to shower." Her steps sound so fucking small as she starts across the living room, heading for the stairs. "I'll let you know my next move after that."

Yeah, I fucked up. Big time.

I stalk across the room and wrap my hand around her arm.

"Don't touch me," she hisses, yanking her arm away.

"Mischief, baby."

"My name is Bella," she growls, spinning to face me with wild eyes. "Not baby. Not little girl. Not Mischief. It's *Bella*."

"Bella, talk to me."

"I think you've said plenty already, Cormac. I'm going upstairs. You can go fly a freaking kite."

She turns to walk away from me again, and what little patience I have left vanishes in a puff of smoke. Her attitude is sexy as hell, but she doesn't give an inch when she's pissed. I deserve it. I shouldn't have yelled at her. But I can't fix it if she won't let me.

I hook an arm around her waist, dragging her back into my arms before she can plant a foot on the first step. She hisses like an angry little kitten, aiming her heel at my shin. I manage to pry the bags out of her hands and dodge her kick at the same time.

The bags hit the floor with a dull thud as I spin her around and haul her up over my shoulder.

"Cormac, you asshole!" she yells, trying to kick me again. "Let me go!"

"No," I growl, planting my hand on her ass to keep her still as I stomp toward the couch with her over my shoulder. "Not until you settle your little ass down and listen to me."

Surprisingly, she doesn't fight me. She doesn't say anything at all. She goes limp, the fight draining out of her. And then I feel her body shake.

My heart plummets into my soles. She's crying.

I made her cry.

"Baby, no," I breathe, quickly pulling her back down into my arms.

"Leave me alone, Cormac," she growls, trying to shake me off as her bottom lip quivers and two big tears roll down her cheeks.

To hell with that, though. I'm not going anywhere, and neither is she.

"Let me go," she pleads, her voice ragged and brittle. More vulnerable than it's ever been.

"No."

What little composure she has left cracks. A sob escapes her lips, shattering my heart.

I scoop her up as she falls apart in my arms, crying like I'm guessing she hasn't cried since she watched her boss die. She clings to me, her face buried in my throat as tears pour down her face and her little body shakes with the force of her cries. Every sob leaves me howling for blood and mad as hell at myself.

"I'm sorry," I croon, cradling her close as she purges herself of the trauma. "It's okay, baby. I'm right here, and you're safe now. Everything is going to be okay."

She tries to say something, but it just sounds like gibberish to me.

I hold her and croon to her, wishing like hell we could go back ten minutes and start over. I'm not supposed to be the motherfucker who makes this goddess cry. If there is a guidebook to getting someone to fall in love with you, I'm almost certain that's item number one. I've listened to my brothers say the same shit for the last year and a half. Never be the reason for their tears.

Crash crawls closer, laying his head against her thigh. He whines low in his throat, looking at me as if to ask what the fuck I did and why the fuck I haven't fixed it yet and made her smile again. It's a sad day when even the dog knows you fucked up.

It takes a good half hour for Bella to cry herself out. When she finally does, she lies quietly in my arms, shudders still wracking her body periodically.

"My dad d-didn't send me here because he was afraid that he couldn't p-protect me from them," she whispers, her voice muffled. "He s-sent me because he was afraid that he c-couldn't protect me f-from m-me." Her warm breath pelts my skin as she sighs sadly. "He didn't trust me not to do something stupid."

"Your dad loves you, Mischief." I know that much for a fact. I talked to the man. He's beside himself with worry, terrified out of his mind that he's going to lose his daughter. He sent her here because he needs her safe.

"I know that." She lifts her head, breathtaking in her sorrow. "But two things can be true at the same time, Cormac." She gives me a sad smile. "To him, I'll always be the headstrong little girl who goes looking for trouble. That's what he expected me to do this time...go looking for trouble. He sent me here to make sure I couldn't do that. I didn't even get a chance to prove I wouldn't."

Shit. No wonder she feels like this is a prison.

And I told her she needs fucking permission to take the dog outside.

I *am* an asshole. But this asshole can be taught.

"I'm not your dad, Bella," I murmur, gently wiping her face.

"You thought I ran off."

"I wasn't worried about you looking for trouble." I exhale a breath. Maybe I should have been, but shit, I'm the last motherfucker to judge someone for looking for trouble when that's all I do. I suppose the fact that she's the same way is divine providence. God is probably yukking it up right now, just waiting to see how karma bites me in the ass with this girl for the thirty-five years of hell I've raised.

I can tell by her expression that she doesn't believe me.

"You matter to me," I say, laying my cards on the table. "I've been waiting for you my entire life. I'm trying to give you time to get on the same page, but I'm an impatient bastard. Going slow with you is hard as hell when I want everything, and I want it right now. I was worried I pushed too far, too soon, and you bolted on me."

"Oh," she whispers, her red-rimmed eyes searching across my face.

"And then I was worried as hell that something might have happened to you. There's a ravine about a mile behind the house. It's half a mile deep. If you were to fall into that...."

Her face pales, understanding dawning.

"And then I thought about someone grabbing you off the road and stuffing you into the trunk." I tip my head back, expelling a slow breath as my blood pressure rises again at the mere thought. "I went through about fifteen different ways I could have lost you, Mischief. It fucked me up a little bit."

"I'm sorry," she whispers.

I tilt my head forward again. "You have nothing to be sorry about. You aren't a prisoner here. You're allowed to go outside without permission. Of course you are."

"I tried to kick you."

"I already told you, baby," I growl, tucking ringlets behind her ears. "Defy me. Fight me. All you do is make my goddamn cock hard when you do."

The color in her cheeks deepens to a dusty rose.

"I wasn't made for a soft woman, Mischief." I shoot her a grin. "And you damn sure weren't made for a weak-ass man."

She rolls her eyes, making me smile. That right there is exactly what I mean, though. This girl is full of fire, full of sass. It spills out of her, barely contained. A soft man couldn't handle her. She needs someone who understands her and what she needs, someone who won't clip her wings or make her less to make himself feel like more. She doesn't fit neatly into a box. Any man who doesn't understand that isn't worthy of her time.

"I'm the one who owes you an apology, Mischief. Worrying about you doesn't excuse the fact that I yelled at you," I murmur regretfully. "I'm so damn sorry for that. Can we please start over?"

"No."

My heart twists in my chest, and my stomach knots up.

"I don't want to start over," she whispers. "I...like the way things are now." Worry casts a shadow in her expression, darkening her eyes. "But I'm not here forever, Tiny. As soon as they catch the men who killed Bellamy, I'm going back to Tennessee."

I'm not sure if she's trying to convince herself or if she's trying to convince me, but I'm not buying what she's selling, and I don't think she is either. I think she knows her home is here now, but she isn't entirely done fighting that fact yet. That's all right, though.

We've got time, and I was built for war.

This little goddess isn't going anywhere.

Chapter Six

Bella

"How did you end up here?" I ask, rubbing Crash's ear between my fingers while Cormac works on lighting the grill. Callum, Andreas, and Catriona are coming for dinner. I think Cormac invited them to give me company.

He still feels guilty for yelling at me yesterday. It's not really his fault that I cried, though. I've been trying to hold off the storm for far too long already. It was bound to happen sooner or later.

The sad fact is I'm kind of a mess right now. The last week of my life feels like a runaway train barreling toward some conclusion I can't see. I'm not used to not being in control. I'm not used to feeling helpless. Quite frankly, it sucks.

I feel like a little girl again, watching my world slowly descend into chaos.

Back then, our dad tried so hard to shield us from the worst of it. But he couldn't hide the fact that reporters followed us. He couldn't hide the whispers from kids at school. We knew a lot more about what Marion did than we should have. We kept a lot of the truth from him, trying to shield him too. But it wasn't easy.

I don't like feeling helpless again now.

"Tate," Cormac murmurs.

"Tate?"

"The Nashville Predators have been regular clients since my dad and uncles started the business, and his uncle was a Predator," he says. "When Bender and Angel needed security, his uncle recommended my family."

"My Aunt Stella's sister is married to a former Predator."

"Yeah?" Cormac pours lighter fluid onto the grill, glancing at me over his shoulder.

"I guess there really aren't any strangers in the south, huh?" I say, smiling.

"Nah, baby. It's just further proof that you and I were meant to be," he says, tossing a match onto the grill. The lighter fluid catches with a whoosh, sending flames up toward the sky. Cormac jumps back with a startled curse.

"What did you expect to happen?" I ask through laughter. "You used half a thing of lighter fluid."

He turns a devastating smirk on me, flashing those dimples. "I like fire."

"And I like edible steak."

"You questioning my grilling abilities, little girl?"

"Um, did you miss the giant flame that just singed your eyebrows off?"

He immediately reaches up to check his eyebrows and then growls at me when he realizes they're both still fully intact. He abandons the grill, stalking across the back deck toward me. The wood vibrates beneath his heavy steps.

"What are you doing?" I ask, breathless at the intense gleam in his eyes.

"Coming to kiss that fucking smile off your face."

"Cormac," I whisper.

"Say my name like that again, and our guests are going to see some things they definitely aren't going to survive seeing, Mischief," he growls. His gaze prowls down my body. "You fell asleep on the couch last night. I didn't get to kiss Snoopy goodnight."

Oh. Wow. It's entirely possible to orgasm without being touched.

"Cormac."

He snarls, lunging for me. Somehow, I end up in his arms with my legs around his waist and my back against the wall. His gray eyes bore into mine, his upper lip curled back from his teeth. His breath comes in harsh pants.

"You laugh, and the fucking angels sing, Mischief."

"Shut up and kiss me, Tiny."

"Nah. You kiss me this time."

I spear my hands into his hair, eagerly dragging his mouth down to mine. All day, I've been dying for another taste of him. But he's been on his best behavior today. We went for a walk earlier, and he showed me where the ravine is. He also showed me an emergency escape route off the property. I think he's trying to prove that he trusts me.

Instead, he's making me fall in love with him. It's terrifying. I'm not supposed to love him. I'm not supposed to want to stay right here in this bubble with him. And yet...and yet I do. My life is in Tennessee. That's always been my home. Except the longer I'm here, the more this begins to feel like home. The more *he* begins to feel like home.

If any part of Marion exists in me, I'm terrified it's going to rear its ugly head and destroy everything. What if I fall too hard? What if I need him too much? What if love makes me ugly and bitter and hateful as it made her? I don't want to be those things. God help me, I want to be his Mischief. Just his.

His tongue touches mine, and my fears fall quiet again, silenced by the power of his kiss, by the intensity of his touch. By the power of *him*. I drag him closer, moaning into his mouth, desperate for more of him. I want the feel of him seared into my brain, the imprint of his hands branded into my flesh. I want him all over me so when he's not there, I still feel him.

"Goddamn, Bella," he growls, bucking his hips into mine when I bite his bottom lip. "I'm going to tear Snoopy from your perfect body if you keep it up."

"I'm not wearing Snoopy today."

"Who?" he demands.

"Maybe I'm not wearing panties at all."

His eyes narrow, hot possession sweeping through them. "You better have my pussy covered, little girl," he growls, pinning my hips to the wall with his as he leans back, readjusting me with his hands around my waist. Once I'm where he wants me, he grabs the band of my leggings—a black pair with little stars on them that the wives picked out for me—and starts rolling it down.

"Cormac, we're outside," I hiss.

"Should have thought of that before you started fucking with me," he rumbles. "Now you're going to sit your pretty ass right there and let me see for myself."

It should be criminal to be this damn bossy and this damn hot at the same time. I don't even like bossy men! But this one gets all growly and starts telling me what I'm going to do, and part of me *wants* to obey him. The other part wants to defy him just to see how he reacts.

He drags the front of my pants down, exposing my panties.

"Jesus Christ," he breathes, his eyes locked on the sheer lace. "This isn't a fucking cartoon, Mischief."

"The wives bought them."

"I can see your cunt."

I moan, my core clenching at the reverent way he says it, as if he's talking about the holy grail.

"Fuck. Tell me I can touch it."

"T-touch me."

He shoves his hand down my panties, tearing the delicate lace.

I bite my tongue, trying to keep from shouting his name into the wild.

"Yo, fucker! You back here?"

I jump as Callum's voice sounds around the side of the house.

Crash starts barking and launches himself off the porch.

Cormac presses his forehead to mine, snarling curses. His eyes meet mine, fury burning bright in the gray depths. "This isn't over," he growls, touching his thumb to my clit. "As soon as they leave tonight, I'm eating my dessert, Mischief."

"Okay," I whisper.

He presses a hard kiss to my mouth and then quickly pulls his hand from my panties and straightens my clothes. He barely has me back on my feet before Callum rounds the side of the house, coming into view. Crash trots along at his side, a giant bone in his mouth.

"Stop bribing my fucking dog to let you on my property," Cormac growls at his cousin.

"Settle down, fucker. I brought you a bribe, too," Callum mutters, holding up a six-pack of beer. His gaze comes to me as he jogs up the steps. "Bella."

"Callum."

He sets the beer on the table and then crosses to me, holding out a shopping bag.

"What's this?" I ask, eyeing him suspiciously.

"Plane snacks," he mutters. "Cormac said I had to replace yours."

I open the bag and peer in, and then blink rapidly. It's overflowing with bags of plane snacks. "Uh, Callum? Did you rob a flight attendant?"

He cracks a smile. "Don't ask what I had to do to get those. You don't want to know."

I laugh, unable to help myself. Maybe Callum isn't so bad after all.

"Great," Cormac mutters from behind me, resignation heavy in his voice. "Now I have to kill my favorite fucking cousin."

"Cormac, what are you–?"

"Pants off," he growls, flipping the lock on the front door and then yanking his shirt off over his head. "Now, Mischief."

"You just slammed the door on Andreas!"

"I don't fucking care. Pants off, baby." He stalks toward me, an implacable beast on the hunt. His eyes are dark, his chest heaving with exertion. He's so damn sexy. Jesus, this man is freaking gorgeous when he's turned on. And he's been turned on all damn night. Every time I looked at him, he was watching me as if he couldn't look away.

Everyone noticed, but he didn't care. I don't think Cormac cares what anything thinks about him or us or his life. He is who he is, and he makes no apologies for it. He isn't cocky or arrogant. He's just...Cormac. He's a category unto himself.

I back toward the couch, not sure if I want to try to get away or if I want to let him have his way with me here and now. Both. Fighting this man is like a drug. God help me, but I love that he lets me do it. He doesn't back down, and he doesn't get fed up. He lets me be who I am and fight him and push his buttons, and he loves every minute of it. No one has ever done that for me before. No one has ever accepted me so completely. I've always been too much, too independent, too fierce to get past a first date. Not with this man.

With him, I'm just enough. And that makes me feel powerful in a way I never have before, secure in a way I've never felt. I can submit to him without becoming less. I can let go for a little while without feeling like I have to settle or give up part of myself to do it. I can be all of me with him. There's something addicting in that too. There's a freedom to it I've never felt.

"One," he growls.

"Why are you counting?"

"Because if you aren't naked when I get to five, I'm ripping those pretty clothes off your body."

"You better not!" I take another step away from him.

"Strip, Mischief."

"I'm serious, Cormac!"

"So am I. Two." He paces toward me.

I back up again, casting a glance to the side to check for an escape route.

"Three."

There's no way I can outrun him, but I'm going to try anyway.

"Four," he growls.

I feint to the left. As soon as he moves that way, I shout, "Five!" and then dodge right, racing toward the stairs.

He curses, and then I hear him chasing behind me. My heart races, adrenaline pumping through my system as I run as hard as I can. Somehow, I make it to the stairs. My feet fly up the steps. His heavier steps sound behind me, so close I know he's gaining ground. Jeez, he's fast for a freaking giant. Probably because he can skip entire freaking steps while I have to take each one. It's cheating, really.

I hit the landing at a dead sprint, racing toward the bedroom.

I'm not even a foot from the door when he catches me.

"No!" I shout as he hauls me up into his arms, pinning my arms to keep me still.

"Caught you," he growls in my ear before delivering a stinging bite.

My stomach bottoms out, heat surging through me in a pyroclastic blast. I think we both know I wanted him to catch me. We also know I'll never admit it. I struggle in his arms, trying to get free even though we both also know that isn't going to happen.

He stomps toward the bedroom, kicking the door closed to keep Crash from interrupting what he's about to do to me. I bounce when I land on the bed, my hair tangled around my face, momentarily blinding me.

I don't even have time to battle it out of the way before he's on me.

My shirt goes first, ripped from my body like paper.

"Don't you dare rip this bra, Cormac Carmichael," I hiss. "They're expensive."

The jerk holds my gaze while he rips it right down the middle.

"You did not," I growl, not entirely surprised. No one tells Cormac what to do.

"Did it. Enjoyed it. Would do it again." The jerk has the audacity to smirk at me before he leans down and wraps that wicked tongue around my nipple.

I shout his name, my back bowing off the bed.

"That's more like it, Mischief. Those are the sounds I want to hear in this bed," he growls, blowing on my nipple. And then he bites it.

"Cormac!" I sob, clawing at his shoulders as a blast of pleasure rips through me.

He does the same thing to the other nipple before leaving a red mark beside it.

"Damn," he breathes, leaning back to look at his handiwork. "You look good wearing my mark, Bella. Might just have to leave them all over this perfect body so everyone knows you belong to me."

"Do I get to mark you too, then?" I demand, staring up at him through a fog of lust.

"Fuck yeah." His eyes light up at the thought. "Mark me, Mischief. Brand me with your name so everyone knows I'm yours. You think I won't wear that shit with pride?" He runs his lips down my stomach, his eyes locked on mine. "Think again, little girl."

He pries my legs apart, fitting his big body between them.

Color blooms in my cheeks, my insides liquefying when he shoves his nose against my mound, inhaling deeply.

"Fuck, I can smell how wet you are, Bella."

"It's your fault," I mutter.

"Then I guess it's a good thing I'm going to fix it, huh?"

I watch with a slack jaw as he rips the crotch out of my pants. He doesn't even try to remove them like a normal person! He just Hulks his way through them like a crazy man.

"I'm so mad at you right now."

"Yeah? Is that why your panties are soaked through? Because you're so mad?" He turns that pirate smile on me, touching his finger to the seam of my panties. "They're drenched, baby."

"Still mad," I say, even though I'm pretty sure I'm lying. It's impossible to be mad at someone who looks at you like he'd crawl through hell for a single taste of you. And that's precisely how Cormac is looking at me right now. I think...Lord, I think this man is in love with me.

And I don't think it's the kind that dies or diminishes or fades, either. It's the kind my dad has with Jenna. The wild, deep kind that endures and grows stronger. The kind Marion was never capable of feeling.

Is that what's beating in my chest right now, threatening to burst out of it? Wild, crazy love for this man? Is that why the thought of leaving him hurts? Is that why he feels like home? Because I'm in love with him? I think...Oh my gosh. I think it is.

I'm in love with Cormac Carmichael. Madly, desperately, wildly in love.

"Cormac, I...."

He grips my panties in his hand and twists, ripping them away from my center.

"Oh, Mischief," he breathes, parting my lower lips with two fingers. "Dessert looks damn good, baby."

His name gets tangled up in my throat, choking me as he takes his first lick. Pleasure bursts to life in vivid, singing color, brighter than anything I've ever seen, more boundless than anything I've ever known. I throw my head back, arching upward.

He growls and licks me again.

I sob wordlessly, caught in a net of intense pleasure that only grows tighter.

He drags me closer to his eager mouth, snarling and greedy. "Goddamn," he mumbles between long licks. "I'm never going to stop eating this perfect cunt." He spreads me wider and licks me again. "So wet. So sweet." His tongue circles my clit, maddeningly slow. "Ah, hell. Look at how pink it is." He thrusts his tongue into my hole, jiggling it there. "It's mine. All goddamn mine."

"Cormac," I moan, not sure what's hotter: the way he mumbles to himself while he eats me or the way he eats me. Both, I think. It's like he's having a religious experience between my legs. He drives his hips into the bed, grinding his erection against the mattress in search of relief as he takes his time, savoring me.

"You want to come, Mischief?" His gray eyes flit to mine.

"Yes!" I sob.

"You're lucky I want to taste it, or I'd keep you just like this for hours. Next time you run from me, I'll be planting my kid in you when I catch you," he growls, dragging my legs over his shoulders. "Remember that, little girl. I'm letting you off easy this time." He runs his tongue around my clit again. "You don't run from me unless you want to pay the price."

"Cormac?" I wait until he meets my gaze again. "What if I want to pay the price?"

He snaps like a cord, heat flaring so hot in his eyes they scorch me. He growls, driving his hips into the mattress hard enough to bounce me upward. I land with his head buried between my legs. He doesn't take his time this time. He eats me like a man pushed too far, growling as he opens his mouth over my center and attacks me with his lips and tongue.

I shout his name, sobbing it into the room.

Crash barks outside the bedroom, pawing at the door.

Cormac spears his tongue into me, stiffening it as he tries to force it deeper. His nose grinds against my clit. I sob, rocking against his face as wave after wave of pleasure blasts through me. They split me wide open, drowning me in bliss.

I come with a sharp cry, clinging to the mattress to keep myself from shattering into pieces too tiny to put back together. Neon lights dance behind my eyelids in a frenzied ballet. Cormac roars my name and then I feel him moving. I peel my eyes open in time to see him straddling my legs, his erection in his fist, his eyes locked on me as he jerks himself off.

Hot ropes of sticky cum jet from his cock, landing against my belly and thighs.

I moan, aftershocks rolling through me as I watch him tremble and shake, moaning my name. He's so damn fierce, so damn beautiful. I never stood a chance with him. From the moment I set eyes on him, falling was inevitable.

And yet...it didn't feel like falling at all.

He held me the whole way down, just like he said he would.

Chapter Seven

Giant

"I have a surprise for you."

Bella glances up from her book, her eyes narrowed in suspicion. "You said that yesterday too, Tiny," she reminds me. "And then you dragged me out of bed and made me go running in the woods."

"I didn't make you go running in the woods," I protest through laughter. "We went for a walk."

She purses her lips and widens her eyes, looking at my legs and then at hers, and then back at mine. "You have about three times more leg than I do. You were out for a casual stroll. *I* was running for my life."

"It took us an hour to go a mile, Mischief."

"Revisionist history," she scoffs.

I shake my head and steal her book, marking her place before I set it aside. "Get your little ass up, and let's go."

"Do I have to walk anywhere?" she asks, making air quotes around the word *walk*.

"Yeah, your happy ass to the garage to get on my bike," I growl, hauling her off the couch to her feet. I press a hard kiss to her mouth and then smack her ass. "Go find your shoes."

"We're taking your bike?" Her eyes light up.

Of course that gets her moving.

She makes a beeline for the stairs, disappearing up them at record speed. I watch her go, smiling like a fucking loon. I swear to Christ, I've never been this goddamn content in my life. For the first time, I feel like my purpose is right here in front of me. I know what I'm meant to do with my life now. I know exactly where I'm supposed to be. I was put on this earth to love this wild woman.

Every damn minute I spend with her, I fall deeper. I love her harder. It's sickening, really. No wonder my brothers are insufferable shiny, happy people all the goddamn time. No wonder they wanted to murder me every time I flirted with their wives. Just the thought of one of them teasing Bella like I teased their wives makes me homicidal.

I probably owe them apologies. Not that the fuckers are getting them or anything. They've been insufferable shiny, happy people. And they've been getting laid regularly. I've been sleeping alone for a year and a half while Bella existed in another state. That's punishment enough for my pain-in-the-ass ways.

Crash butts his head against my thigh, silently demanding attention.

I lean down to scratch his ears.

"You're staying behind again today, buddy," I murmur, breaking the bad news to him. "I need you to keep an eye on shit here."

He huffs out a breath, glancing toward the stairs.

"I'll bring her back," I promise. He's obsessed with her. When it's just the two of us, he sleeps on the couch. With Bella here, he sleeps in the bedroom. I had to put a blanket down on her side of the bed to keep him off the bed. He sleeps right beside her, watching over her.

She's been sleeping peacefully for the most part. When she drifts too far away, the nightmares start. As soon as I get her back in my arms, her mind settles. We haven't talked about it again since the first night, but I think she knows there's a reason for that. She belongs here with me, plain and simple.

Mac Sterling isn't going to like it, but that's too bad for him. She's mine to care for now. If she really wants to move back to Tennessee, I'll go with her. Whatever she needs to be happy. But one way or another, her future is with me. I don't care if that's here or if it's there so long as she's with me where she belongs.

Though, truthfully, I'm hoping she'll want to stay here at least part-time. The last thing I want to do is split up her and her twin, but Silver Spoon Falls is home for me. The place is in my blood. When I envision my future, it's always been here.

"I'm ready, Tiny."

I glance up to watch her bounce down the stairs. Well, I watch her tits bounce.

She lands at the bottom like an angel, smiling sweetly. "Where are we going?"

Hacker has us a secure line so she can video chat with her family, but I decide not to tell her. If anything goes wrong between here and there and we have to reschedule the call, I don't want to break her heart. She's had it broken far too many times already. But I hope like hell we don't have to reschedule, and she can talk to her family today. She needs to hear from her sister. Thinking she's mad at her is weighing heavily on my girl. The tension between her and Mac is weighing on her too. Until they hash their shit out, she won't be able to settle.

"You'll see," I say, reaching for her hand.

Crash whines, a mournful, self-pitying sound.

"Aww, Crash," Mischief coos, stopping to scratch his ears. "Keep the couch warm for me, big guy. We'll be back soon to hang out."

Crash rolls his eyes to the side, giving me a look full of satisfaction. My goddamn dog is a con artist. Not that I blame him or anything. Maybe I should take a page from his book and pout so she rubs on me. It's a plan with definite merit.

"Where are we going? What are we doing?" she peppers me with questions all the way to the garage. And while we mount the bike. I'm pretty sure she's still asking them when we take off. She's relentless and eager. I fucking love it. Despite everything she's been through, she's still fearless and curious, her spirit untamed.

When I pull up in front of Hacker's office fifteen minutes later, he's waiting out front. I park across two spaces in the parking lot and then stand to steady the bike for Bella to dismount. She swings her leg over and hops gracefully to the ground, already working on the strap beneath her chin to remove the helmet.

"Where are we?" she asks as soon as it's off, looking all around.

Hacker's office is crammed between a boutique and a doctor's office. There are no signs out front, nothing that states what the building is or what type of business is conducted within. The glass windows are tinted so dark you can't see through them, and everything is locked up tighter than Fort Knox. He has millions of dollars of computer equipment inside, and access to God only knows how many top-secret systems.

"Hacker's office," I murmur, nodding to my brother.

She spins to face me, her eyes wide and hopeful. "Did he...?"

"Let's go see, Mischief."

She grabs my hand, practically dragging me the short distance to my MC brother. He pushes away from the wall, meeting us with an amused grin stretched across his face. Like Bella, his girl is a handful, though for entirely different reasons. Scarlett is as sweet as they come, but she came complete with an aunt who keeps this town on its toes. Ms. Ophelia is the original gangster when it comes to hellraising. She keeps Hacker sweating.

"Giant," he says, smirking at me before he turns a smile on my girl. "Hey, sweetheart."

"Her name is Bella," I growl.

She elbows me in the ribs. Hard.

"Jesus Christ, woman."

"Oops. My arm slipped."

Hacker fucking cackles, the bastard.

"Laugh it up," I mutter. "See if I help you chase down Ophelia next time she goes on the lam."

His laughter dries up lickety-split.

"Who is Ophelia?" Mischief asks, eyeing me curiously.

"The coolest old lady you'll ever meet," I say. "She's a badass. You're going to love her when you meet her." Actually, shit. Maybe I shouldn't introduce them. God only knows what the fuck they'll do together.

Nah, I'm definitely introducing them. I can handle any trouble my girl gets into, and she'll love Ophelia. Besides, she deserves to see that there's nothing wrong with the way she is. Ophelia may be a troublemaker, but she's done more for this town than anyone else living in it. Bella needs that kind of role model. She needs to know that she's perfect exactly the way she is and that she doesn't have to change a goddamn thing or fit in any box.

"Cool," she whispers.

I glance from her to Hacker, who jerks his chin in a nod, silently letting me know that we're good to go. I exhale a relieved breath.

"Hacker has you set up to video chat with your family, Mischief," I murmur quietly, tipping her chin up to face me. "If anyone is trying to trace you through them, they won't be able to find you this way."

"I get to video chat with them?"

"Yeah, baby."

Her eyes grow damp as she looks between me and Hacker, gratitude searing her expression. "Thank you," she whispers, her voice shaking.

Hacker leads us inside, using his thumbprint to gain access to the building. The lobby is completely inconspicuous. Blue walls, dark furniture, and hardwood floors give it a lavish, comfortable feel. But there's no hint of what the place is. There's no reception desk, no logo on the wall, nothing.

He stops at the only door out of the lobby, using the retina scanner to open it. A blast of cold air hits us.

Bella shivers.

"Shit." I strip my MC jacket off and wrap it around her shoulders. The damn thing fits her like a dress, but she snuggles into it gratefully. She looks cute as hell. Might just have to get her into my clothes more often.

"Why is it so cold?" she asks.

"Servers," Hacker says, pointing to a row of equipment along the back wall. Lights flicker and flash, and the entire row hums and whirs like a thousand fans running simultaneously. "They generate a lot of heat, so I have to keep it cold to keep them running. If they overheat, it fucks up every other system I've got running."

"Oh."

"Through here," he says, holding open the door to his office.

Bella steps inside, her mouth gaping open when she sees his setup. It's impressive. Two massive, curved monitors are stacked on top of one another, with smaller monitors on each side. He has three different keyboards of various types, about fifteen pieces of equipment that I have no name for, and a mouse neatly arrayed on top of his desk. I fully intend to steal his chair one day. It's comfortable as fuck.

"Holy crap. You're like the freaking Tesla of hacking," Bella mutters

Hacker chuckles, sliding around her to a laptop set up on the edge of the desk. "I get by," he says, all humble and shit. In reality, the man makes millions doing what he does. Everyone from Fortune 500 companies to the federal government has his ass on speed dial. "You'll call on this, Bella."

She drifts closer, listening as he runs through the instructions with her. It's simple, really. He's set the laptop up on a secure line that traces back to some other location. So long as she's connected to the VPN, using the phone number and program he installed, she can chat with her family whenever she wants.

"I'll swing by later to make sure you can access the VPN from home," he says.

She grabs his arm, her eyes wide. "I can talk to them from home?"

I growl, a low, rumbling sound.

Bella immediately drops her hand from Hacker's arm, jumping back a step. She turns those baby blues on me, damn near bowling me over.

"Sorry," she mouths.

"Possessive asshole," Hacker says without heat.

Ten minutes later, Hacker leaves the office, giving Bella privacy to call her family. She squirms in his chair, trying to get comfortable.

"You're stalling."

"Am not."

"Yeah, you are."

She huffs out an annoyed breath. "I'm nervous. What if Isla is still mad at me?" Her teeth sink into her bottom lip, worrying it. "I don't want her to be mad at me anymore, Tiny."

"Then tell her that, baby." I nudge the laptop toward her. "You'll never know if you don't call."

She grabs my hand, looking up at me. "Will you stay?"

"You want me in here?"

"Yes," she whispers.

"Yeah, I'll stay, Mischief." I press my lips to her forehead in a gentle kiss.

She exhales a breath and presses the button to call her family. I lean back against the wall behind her, trying not to crowd her but sticking close. I want to pick her up and put her in my lap. But I figure Mac and I should have a conversation before I show up onscreen with his baby girl in my lap.

"Pirate Princess!" A curvy blonde woman's smiling face fills the screen, her gaze warm as it runs all over Bella. "Oh, sweetheart. We miss you so much."

"Hi, Mom," Bella whispers. "I miss you too."

"Are you okay, baby girl? Are you giving Cormac trouble?"

"Yes, and yes." A tiny smile curves Bella's lips upward as she glances over her shoulder at me.

Jenna Sterling laughs quietly.

"Of course you're encouraging her," Mac grumbles, coming into the frame. He doesn't seem pissed about it, though. If anything, he seems amused that his daughter is giving me hell. He may worry about her, but he doesn't want to change her. Thank fuck for that.

"Hi, Dad," she whispers, fidgeting.

"Hey, baby girl." He smiles at her and then turns his blue eyes on me. Unlike his daughter, Mac Sterling isn't cuddly and sweet. He's a man with a daughter to protect, and I'm a motherfucker with a cock. He made the rules clear before he sent her here. "Cormac."

"Mac," I say, inclining my head.

He narrows his eyes on me, looking between me and his daughter. I don't know what he sees or if it's just fatherly intuition, but he fucking knows. "Son of a bitch," he curses, scowling. "You and I had a fucking agreement, Carmichael."

"Things changed."

"Change them back," he growls. "I didn't send my daughter to you to keep your bed warm."

"That's not even what's happening," I growl.

"Daddy!" Bella gasps at the same time.

"Mac," Jenna says, placing a hand on her husband's arm.

"No? She's there a few weeks, tops. Your entire life is there."

"Maybe mine is too!" Bella cries, shocking everyone. Shocking me. Jesus, I hope she means it. "You chose for me when you decided to send me here, but you don't get to decide this for me too. I love you, but this is my life and my decision, not yours."

"Bella, baby girl," Mac says.

"No, daddy." She throws up a hand. "You didn't trust me to keep myself out of trouble. Trust me now. Cormac is a *good* man. I know this because one of the best raised me."

"Jesus," Mac growls, scrubbing a hand down his face. His eyes come to me. For a long moment, he doesn't say anything. And then he curses. "You better take care of her or you'll be removing my goddamn boot from your ass."

"He'll have to remove mine first," Bella says sweetly.

"That's my girl," Jenna whispers.

CHAPTER EIGHT

Bella

"H i," Isla says, slipping into Mom's chair as she and my dad leave the room with our younger siblings to give us privacy.

"Hi," I whisper, reaching blindly for Cormac's hand. He grips mine, silently lacing our fingers together. "Um, this is Cormac."

She doesn't know about him yet. She only came in at the tail end of my conversation with the rest of the family. I was worried she wasn't going to come at all.

"I've heard a lot about you, Isla," Cormac says. "It's nice to see you."

Isla's gaze drifts to him, her eyes going wide as she takes him in. "Whoa," she says after a minute. "What did they feed you?"

I giggle, the knots in my stomach unraveling as Cormac chuckles. "I wondered the same thing!"

Isla cracks a smile.

"I'm sorry," we blurt at the same time.

My twin shifts restlessly, her expression slipping into one of pure misery. "Are you very mad at me?" she asks, chewing on her bottom lip.

"Mad at you? You were mad at me!"

"No, I wasn't."

"Yes, you were."

"Was not."

"Were too."

She opens her mouth to argue and then laughs ruefully. "Are we really arguing over who was mad at who?"

"I...." I grimace. "Yeah, that's pretty dumb."

She laughs again, and then glances at Cormac. She doesn't say anything, but she doesn't have to say it. She's my best friend, and my twin. I know what she's thinking before she does half the time.

"Can you give us a minute, Tiny?"

"Shit. Yeah." He leans down, brushing a gentle kiss across my lips. "I'll be right outside, baby."

"Okay."

He exits the office, pulling the door closed behind him.

"Baby?" Isla squeaks, her eyes comically wide. "Holy crap, Bella. He just kissed you. And you let him!"

"I know," I whisper, pressing my hands to my cheeks. I stare at her. "I think I'm in love with him."

"I freaking knew it!" Isla squeals. "You look different. Happy."

"I am happy." I swallow hard. "And scared out of my mind."

"Why?"

I shrug instead of answering.

"Why, Bella?"

"What if I'm like Marion?" I whisper, tears welling in my eyes. "What if I'm selfish and terrible and jealous, and I destroy his life?"

"Bella," Isla says, her expression falling.

"I could be like her. Maybe that's why I'm always causing problems. Because I'm like her."

"You *aren't*," Isla whispers fiercely, wiping her eyes. "You've always been brave and fierce and put everyone else first. Your problem has never been that you don't know how to love. It's never been that you're selfish or terrible or jealous. You're the least selfish person I know."

"I don't want to mess this up."

"You can't mess up love, Bella."

"Marion did," I remind her.

"Mom...Marion...didn't love our dad, not really. She didn't know how to love him. She was just an insecure, unhappy girl who thought he was her ticket to a better life. She loved the idea of him," Isla says with a sad smile. "She didn't even know him. If she had, she would have known that the way she treated us destroyed any chance she ever had of winning his heart."

She's not wrong. Our dad loves us fiercely. As soon as Marion started neglecting us, she lost our dad. He tried to make their marriage work because he felt like he owed her that much, but any softer feelings he had for her died the first time her jealousy and selfishness hurt us.

"You don't have to do that, you know," I whisper, dabbing at my eyes with the sleeve of Cormac's jacket. It smells like him, and that gives me strength. *He* gives me strength. I don't feel like a problem with him. He makes me feel as if I'm exactly who I'm supposed to be.

"Do what?" Isla's brows furrow in confusion.

"Call her Marion. You're allowed to call her mom. Just because I don't doesn't mean you can't," I say.

"I know," she whispers. "It's just weird. She's trying to be a better person, and I want to give her that chance. I want to forgive her, but Jenna is our mom, you know? Marion never wanted us. I can't help but think she only wants us now because she's lonely and has no one else."

"Maybe, or maybe she's tired of being a problem too."

"*You* aren't a problem."

I smile, more grateful for my twin than I know how to put into words. "I miss you."

"I miss you too." She frowns. "But don't you dare think about coming back here because of me, Bella. If your heart is there, that's where you belong. Once it's safe, I'll come visit. And you can come to visit. We'll make Uncle Ian put that ridiculous private plane to use every week if that's what it takes."

"Promise?"

"Pinky promise." She touches her pinky to the monitor and then waits for me to do the same. "I should go. You have *things* to do."

We both giggle.

"Wait. What did you want to talk about?" I ask before she can end the chat.

"What? Oh." She waves a hand in the air in a dismissive gesture. "It's nothing. We can talk about it next time."

I narrow my eyes, suspicious. One thing Isla is not is a good liar. She's hiding something. But she blows me a kiss and quickly ends the chat with a rushed, "Love you!" before I can demand answers.

I close the lid on the laptop and then sit there for several long moments, replaying our conversation. For the first time in days, I feel completely whole. As if all the missing pieces of me have stitched themselves back together.

Isla isn't angry with me. My dad and I are...well, he's not on a plane right now. He's giving me space to make my own decisions and choices, even knowing that choice could mean losing me to a bossy giant in Texas.

I never imagined I'd want to stay when I got on the plane to come here, but I never expected to run headfirst into love with my bodyguard either. My family is in Tennessee...but my heart is here. Maybe I'll be bad at love. Maybe I am all the things I fear. But maybe, like Isla says, I'm none of those things.

I want to find out.

When we get home, I'm telling Cormac how I feel about him. I'm diving in with both feet.

"Where are we?" I ask, lifting the helmet off my head and staring in wonder at the waterfall cascading down into a clear blue lagoon. A thick tangle of trees grows all around us, shutting out the rest of the world.

"The Falls," he murmurs, climbing off the bike behind me. He wraps an arm around my waist, dragging me back against his chest. His lips touch the side of my throat. "This place is magic."

I can believe it. It's a perfect oasis of tranquility, far removed from the activity of the sprawling town.

"It's beautiful."

"I'm serious," he murmurs against my throat. "The water is magic."

I turn to look at him over my shoulder.

"It brought you to me."

"Uh, I'm pretty sure a plane and your cousin did that, Tiny."

"Nope." He nips my throat, slipping his hand beneath the hem of my shirt to splay it across my belly. "The water in this town did. I've been drinking gallons of the shit, waiting for it to bring my soulmate to me." He inches his hand upward to cup my breast. "Now you're here. Magic."

I moan, dropping my head back against his chest. I'm pretty sure he's crazy, but I don't care. We can be crazy together.

"Now, I gotta get you on the same page as me," he says. "Get naked and swim with me, Mischief."

My eyes flutter open. "Here? Now?"

"Scared?" he taunts, one brow arched.

Even though I know exactly what he's doing, it freaking works. My heart rebels at the label, refusing to wear it.

"Of your magic water?" I scoff, yanking my shirt off over my head. "Never."

His eyes heat and darken, turning my favorite shade of gunmetal gray. I never knew that color could be so damn erotic, yet it is. He wears it like sin.

He pulls his shirt off, dropping it beside mine. My bra goes next, followed by his belt. Neither of us speaks as we strip one article of clothing at a time, our eyes locked on one another in a silent battle that's more communion than war.

There's a reason why this man drives me wild. My soul recognizes his. His was made for mine. He's my perfect match in every way. Sin drips from his lips, and trouble dances in his eyes, the same way it does in mine. We're two sides of the same coin, a cosmic duality in the flesh.

"Brave little goddess," he growls, dragging me into his arms for a searing kiss once we're stripped bare to the elements. His erection nestles against my stomach, hot and hard. Always so damn hard.

I slip my hand between our bodies, wrapping my fingers around his length.

"Careful, little girl," he growls, his eyes at half-mast. "Your first time will be right here on the bank if you keep that up."

"Yeah? And what if I do this, Tiny?" I sink to my knees in the grass, reaching for him. My fingers trail along his balls as I bring him toward my mouth, eager to taste him like he did me.

"Ah, fuck," he groans, his stomach muscles flexing.

I lick the head of his cock. Moan at the unique, salty taste of him. Run my lips all over the broad head.

He plants his feet, snarling curses.

Oh, I like this.

"Goddamn, Mischief. I knew that sassy fucking mouth was going to blow my mind," he growls, gathering my hair up in his fist as I lick and kiss all over his shaft. "Wrap those pouty lips around me and do your worst, baby. Torture me."

So I do. I plunge down on him, taking him deep into my mouth. My lips stretch to accommodate him. My eyes water. Jesus. He's built like a freaking God. My mouth is full and still, there's so much more.

"Ah, God, yeah." He rocks his hips in gentle pulses, unable to stay still. That's the thing about this man. He's in charge even when he's not. I don't have to hold back because *he* doesn't hold back. We are who we are, and we burn together.

I pull back and then plunge down again, working my hands up toward my mouth at the same time. I want to watch him unravel. I want to be the reason he loses his mind.

"You trying to make me come down that perfect throat, Mischief?"

I bob my head, not denying it.

He groans, pulsing his hips again. Tears leak from the corners of my eyes as he hits the back of my throat.

"Too bad, baby," he says, pulling out of my mouth suddenly. He leans down, yanking me up from the ground.

"When I come again, it'll be in your cunt while I'm planting my kid in you."

"Cormac!" I cry.

He smacks my ass, storming down the bank toward the water. The big jerk doesn't even give me time to prepare before he tosses me.

I sink like a freaking stone, the cool water closing over my head. It's freaking cold! My feet touch the sandy bottom, and I kick off, catapulting myself upward.

I emerge spluttering and trembling to find him wading toward me wearing that pirate smile.

"You are such a jerk," I hiss, battling hair out of my face.

"You were getting too fucking hot," he says, pulling me into his arms.

"I should drown you."

"You could," he murmurs, yanking my legs up around his hips. "But then I couldn't do this." He shoves his hand between us, his thumb zeroing in on my clit.

"Oh!"

"See? You fucking love when I do this, Mischief." His mouth slants down over mine, claiming my lips in a deep kiss.

I grip his shoulders, riding his hand as the water splashes around us. I'm not cold anymore. I'm burning up, spiraling toward an orgasm at the speed of light.

"I love you, Mischief," Cormac whispers right when I'm on the edge.

I shatter like finely spun glass, shouting his name into the sky. Ripples move through me, setting off a tsunami of sensation. One bleeds into the other, each more powerful than the last. But at the very heart of it all is awe.

I come down slowly, floating back to earth in his arms. "Cormac," I whisper, placing one trembling hand against his cheek.

He turns his face into it, kissing my palm.

"You don't need magic water to get me on the same page." I meet his gaze, holding it...letting him see the truth painted across my face. "I'm already there."

His nostrils flare, his pupils dilating.

"I love you."

"Fuck," he growls.

"I was going to tell you when we got home." I take a breath and exhale it slowly. "I'm afraid, though. Um, I've never done this before. I've never wanted this before. I don't want to mess it up."

"I've never done this before either."

"I...wait. Really?"

"I've been waiting for you, Bella."

"Cormac," I whisper.

"You can't mess this up, baby. There's nothing you could possibly do to make me love you less." He presses his forehead to mine. "We're ride or die, little girl. That won't ever change. You're my fucking soul."

"What if I'm jealous?"

"Baby, I'm jealous of the dog when you're scratching his ears," he says, laughing. "I'm jealous of fucking Snoopy for touching my pussy. I'm goddamn jealous Callum brought you plane snacks and made you smile."

"You're crazy." I smile, unable to help myself.

"Yeah, and your little ass made me that way," he growls. "So be jealous, baby. I plan to be jealous as hell when it comes to you. You're fucking mine. I won't ever share you."

"What if I'm a brat?"

He grabs my hand, shoving it between our bodies. "Feel this?" he asks, closing my fingers around his erection. "This is what you do to me every fucking time you cop an attitude. *Please* be a brat. I live for that shit, Mischief."

Well, put that way....

I wrap my hand more firmly around him, squeezing.

"Mischief. I already warned you once," he growls.

"Beds are overrated, Tiny. Make love to me here by your magic water," I whisper, stroking him slowly. "Let's be bad together."

"Jesus Christ. I knew skinny dipping would work," he mumbles, already wading toward shore.

Within moments, we're on the bank, and he's grabbing a blanket from his saddlebag. He unfolds it with a flourish before flipping it onto the thick grass.

"Come here," he murmurs, pulling me back into his arms. "Let me warm you up."

I go willingly, pressing my body to his as he draws me down to the ground. He sits with me in his lap, my legs around his waist.

"You're so damn beautiful, Mischief." He brushes my hair away from my face, leaning down to kiss water droplets from my skin. "Every damn time I look at you, you take my breath away."

"You do too." I trace my fingers over his cheekbones and then down his muscular shoulders. "I never thought I'd fall in love with the freaking Hulk."

"I love that." He gives me those dimples again.

"What?"

"My size is not a bonus where you're concerned." He chuckles. "It annoys the hell out of you."

"Well, yeah." I frown at him. "It's really hard to kick an ass you can barely reach, Tiny."

He laughs again, tipping me over backward so I land on my back beneath him. "That's what I love, Mischief. I'm not a goddamn bucket list item to you. My size isn't something in a checklist. You don't give a shit how big I am. You're going to give me hell and fight me regardless."

"You aren't a bucket list item," I agree, squirming beneath him. "But, um, there is one thing I'd like to check off the list any minute now."

"Yeah? What's that?"

"You inside me."

"Oh, we're getting there, baby," he growls. "But not until I get dessert."

"Cormac," I moan.

"I'm starving for you, Mischief. So lay back and let me have my snack, and then I'll take the cherry you keep waving in my face."

"I do not!"

"Yeah, you do."

His lips close around my nipple, and my argument dissolves. Who needs to argue anyway?

I stare up at the bright blue sky as he tortures me slowly, reducing me to a stuttering, sobbing mess. If anyone else is around, they definitely hear me. They probably see us too. But I don't really care. Part of the thrill is getting caught, and I know Cormac wouldn't have me out here if he didn't think we were completely alone.

He kisses a hot trail down my body, leaving little love bites to mark his journey. I writhe beneath him, pleading for him to go faster. The wicked man doesn't listen, of course.

By the time he finally settles between my legs, beads of sweat replace the water droplets on my skin. He throws my legs over his shoulders, lifting me toward his mouth.

"Fuck, I missed this sweet little thing," he growls, diving right in.

My hips jolt upward, a sharp cry ringing out around us. Filthy sounds fill the air as he eats me, loud and messy and wild. I sob his name, shouting it to the heavens. Nothing should feel this damn good.

And yet it does. So damn good.

I grind my hips against his face, clinging to his hair as he attacks my clit with his tongue. He thrusts two fingers inside me, stretching and fucking me with them, driving me out of my mind.

When I'm on the edge, he pries my cheeks apart. His tongue presses against my back entrance.

I shout his name, shocked.

"I feel your cunt squeezing the fuck out of my fingers, Mischief," he growls, hooking an arm around my waist to drag me back down beneath him. "Don't pretend you don't fucking love having my tongue on this hot little hole."

Oh. God. He's right. I do love it. Maybe I shouldn't, but I do.

"It's mine too. I'll eat it if I want." He buries his face between my cheeks again, circling that hole with his tongue. He stiffens it, forcing the tip of it into me while stroking my g-spot at the same time.

I come apart at the seams, screaming as an orgasm knocks me breathless.

Before it even ends, Cormac picks me up, putting me in his lap again. "I can't wait," he growls, his face wet with my juices and his eyes on fire with need. "Christ, baby. I need to fuck you."

"Yes," I moan.

"Straddle me. I want you wrapped around me while I'm fucking my kid into you."

I wrap my legs around his hips, moaning when the head of his erection grinds against my clit.

"Ah, fuck. You feel like heaven already," he growls like he's mad about it. His teeth sink into the hollow of my shoulder as he notches himself at my entrance.

I rock my hips, eager to get him inside me. I *need* him inside me now.

"Slow, baby," he croons, holding me firmly around the waist. "Slow. It'll kill me if I hurt you."

His confession slows me down and steadies me.

"Cormac," I whisper.

He lifts his gaze to mine.

I sink down slowly, our eyes locked. Neither of us breathes as he fills me. It's heavenly torture, so damn slow the moment seems to last forever as my body stretches around him. And yet it doesn't last long enough either. I want to stay in this moment for eternity, with fierce devotion blazing in his eyes as he claims what belongs to him. As I claim what belongs to me.

"I love you," he whispers.

A tear slips down my cheek.

He wipes it away with the pad of his thumb.

I sink lower, the stretch morphing to discomfort. A small twinge of pain lances through me, and then it's gone, replaced by a curious fullness and intense pleasure. My hips settle against his.

"Fucking fearless," Cormac mutters, leaning up to claim my lips in a hungry kiss. The movement causes his pelvis to grind against my clit.

I jerk, bouncing slightly on his lap.

We both moan in ecstasy.

He tightens his grip on my waist, lifting me slightly. I use my grip on his thighs to drag me back down.

"Fuck," he growls against my lips.

We work together. He lifts me, and then I drag myself back down, sobbing into his mouth as pleasure builds on pleasure, driving me higher.

He lifts me higher. I pull myself back down faster. And then harder. I circle my hips, chasing some instinctive rhythm that seems to sing in my blood.

It sings in his too. He fucks me in time to it, murmuring a litany of praise against my lips.

"So good, so good. Ah, fuck, little girl. You've got my cock so fucking hard. Ride it like you own it. It's yours."

I drag my nails down his back, chanting his name. I never want it to end. And yet I can't hold off the orgasm. He feels too good. His cock dragging against my walls, his panted breaths against my lips, his hard body all over me.

"Cormac," I gasp. "I'm going to come."

"Fuck," he breathes, pure reverence in his tone. "Do it, Mischief. Let me feel it."

I drop down harder, gripping his shoulder to give myself leverage. He doesn't lift me this time. I do it myself, taking what I need from him.

"Yes," he groans, watching me with those gunmetal gray eyes. "Fuck yourself with my cock, baby. Use me to get yourself there. I'm your goddamn toy. Fuck. Use me."

I sob his name, unraveling like a spool of thread. Flames erupt inside my veins, liquefying me. I come hard, crying his name to the heavens.

He roars and rolls us, flipping me to my stomach. His hard body pins me to the blanket as he covers me. I shout in ecstasy as he lets go, driving into me in deep thrusts that impale me on him, threatening to split me open.

It feels so good. So good.

I say it over and over again, babbling it as another orgasm wrecks me.

I don't fall alone. He buries his face in my neck and stills, whispering my name. His sticky seed splashes into me in thick ropes, warming me.

We writhe through it, both silent, both in rapture. Both sated.

He rolls off me, dragging me into his arms. His heart pounds against my back, a joyous, frenetic rhythm. "You were worth the wait," he whispers, his lips at my ear.

"So were you," I whisper back.

"You called my place home today," he says an hour later, helping me dress. "Twice."

"Did I? Weird," I tease, hiding a smile behind my hair.

He growls playfully. "You also broke my rules today."

"Hacker doesn't count as another man, Tiny!"

He cocks a brow.

"You're ridiculous."

He smirks and plops the helmet down on my head. "Get your cute ass on the bike before I decide to spank you anyway."

"Fine, but I'm hungry. You have to take me home this time," I say, emphasizing the word *home*.

His eyes light up, that pirate smile blinding.

Before he can mount the bike, a police cruiser rolls up the gravel lane.

"Shit," Cormac mutters, coming to stand beside me.

The cruiser pulls in beside the bike. The window rolls down. A flipping gorgeous cop about Cormac's age eyes the two of us.

"Got a call about teenagers parked up here, up to no good," he says, his dark gaze inscrutable. "You two know anything about that?"

"Nope," Cormac says. "Haven't seen a teenager, Sheriff."

"What about you?" the Sheriff asks me.

"No," I whisper, my heart pounding.

He grunts, and then his stern facade cracks, and he laughs. "Take your overgrown ass home, Giant. Before Lilah Davis stops calling me and drives out here herself to see something she's too goddamn old to see."

"Already headed that way," Cormac says.

The Sheriff laughs again and then rolls his window up before backing out.

"Someone could see us?" I hiss at Cormac, my cheeks blazing with heat.

"Nah, Mischief. Lilah lives too far away to see." He pauses, that unrepentant pirate smile stealing across his face. "She definitely heard the show, though."

"Oh, my God," I whisper. "I hate you."

He laughs loudly. "No, you don't."

He's right. I don't.

Chapter Nine

Giant

I can't keep my fucking hands off Mischief, and she's more than willing to let me have my way with her at every available opportunity. Three days pass in a sex-fueled haze. As soon as clothes touch her perfect body, I'm removing them again, tearing them from her in my haste to bare her to my touch. It's a good goddamn thing I'm a millionaire because she already needs new shit.

We fuck all over the property. And it's still not enough to sate either one of us. It's still not enough to cool the fire burning between us. Every minute, I fall deeper under her spell. I find some new thing to love about her. Like her irrational disdain of Will Farrell movies. Or the fact that she cries when we watch Beauty and the Beast, only to swear that she had something in her eye. Or how she always sneaks scraps to Crash and then bats those lashes at me and pretends she has no idea what I'm talking about.

She's fierce and beautiful and lives her life fully outside the lines. I never want to give her up. I never want our bubble to pop. Yet far too soon, it does.

I check in with Mac for an update every morning. He's not thrilled that his daughter chose me. I think his daughter could choose Jesus and he'd be pissed about it. But what she said about him not trusting her rattled him. So he bites his tongue. Mostly. He did threaten to bury my body if I break her heart. He won't have to do it though. I'll cut out my own damn heart before I break hers.

The fourth morning after our visit to the Falls, my phone rings at the ass crack of dawn. I quickly silence it to keep from waking Mischief, and then roll out of bed, concerned when I see Mac's number on the display. He never calls me directly. We've been using Hacker's secure line all week as an extra safety precaution.

Crash lifts his head to look at me, and then decides to steal my spot in the bed. He plops down beside Bella with a grunt, closing his eyes. Damn spoiled dog.

"What's up?" I ask, ducking out into the hallway to talk to Mac.

"Has Bella heard from Isla?" he growls, tension heavy in his voice. Threads of fear vibrate just below the surface, bringing me fully awake.

"No. They were supposed to talk yesterday but Isla ran out early. She said she had an appointment she forgot about. Why?" I ask.

"Motherfucker," Mac growls. "She's missing."

My stomach sinks like a fucking stone.

"What the fuck do you mean by missing?"

"I mean missing," he snaps. "She left in the middle of the night." His voice cracks. "She left a goddamn note on her pillow saying not to worry, and that she was safe. But her fucking phone is here. Her car is here. I can't track her."

"Jesus Christ," I breathe. Bella is going to freak out. The worst place for Isla right now is running around by herself. She looks too goddamn much like Bella. If the wrong people get their hands on her.... "What do you need?"

"Find my daughter," Mac rasps. "I don't care what it takes. Help me find my daughter."

I don't even hesitate. Bella is here with the MC and my men to protect her. Every last one of them will take a bullet before they let anyone hurt her. But losing her sister will destroy her in ways that can't ever be repaired. They share a bond that time doesn't heal.

"I'll be there by noon," I promise.

"Bella, baby," I whisper, running my hand down the side of her face. "Wake up."

"Go away, Tiny. It's too early for more sex," she mumbles, dragging my pillow closer. "Ask again in ten minutes."

I smile despite myself. She's too damn perfect. I don't want to tell her this. It's going to break her heart.

"Wake up, Mischief. Something happened."

I'm not sure if my words sink in or if something in my tone registers, but her lashes flutter. Those baby blues open, fixating on me.

"Is it bad?" she whispers.

I don't lie to her. I can't.

"I don't know."

She sighs and pulls herself up into a sitting position, dragging the covers with her. "Tell me," she says, as fearless as ever. Bella never wants the comforting lie. She'd rather have the hard truth, plainly spoken.

I hesitate anyway, pulling her into my lap before I give it to her. She rests her head on my shoulder, letting me comfort her even before she knows why.

"Isla is missing," I murmur, giving her the truth the way she wants it. "She left a note on her pillow and left in the middle of the night. No one knows where she's gone."

"Oh, Iz," Bella sighs.

"Do you know where she might go, baby?"

"No." She shakes her head. Hesitates. And then shakes it again.

"Tell me," I demand.

"I don't have anything to tell," she says, brows furrowed as she looks up at me. "She's been acting weird when we talk, like she's holding something back, but she hasn't been ready to talk about it." Her expression falls. "Maybe I should have pushed."

"This isn't your fault," I growl, cupping her cheek. "Don't think it is."

"What if...?"

"We aren't going to let that happen," I say firmly. "I've already called Andreas. He'll have his jet ready to go in an hour. We're going to find her."

"I'll go get dressed." She pushes away from me, rising to her feet on the bed.

I grab her, dragging her back down into my arms. "You aren't going, Mischief."

"What? Yes, I am."

"You aren't."

Her chin comes up, stubborn intractability firing in her eyes. And goddamn. I wish I had time to fuck her happy again, but I don't. There's no time to argue either. The longer we do, the longer Isla is out there unprotected and vulnerable. The longer she's in danger.

I vowed to protect Mischief. That means protecting her heart too. I have to bring her sister home safely. There is no other option. Not one I can live with anyway. Not one she can, either.

"You aren't the boss of me, Cormac Carmichael. I'm going home to find my sister," she growls.

"No, baby, you aren't. Putting yourself in danger won't get her out of it. You're already home. And you're going to keep your stubborn little ass right here where you belong while I go find your sister." I narrow my eyes on her, not fucking around this time. "I'll tie you to this bed if that's what it takes."

"You wouldn't."

"You know damn well that I would."

"If you tie me up, I'll never forgive you," she cries, betrayal stamped across her face as she hurriedly puts distance between us. Seeing the pain in her eyes fucking kills me. Knowing she's mad at me kills me too. It's a goddamn miserable position to be in, hurting the woman you live and breathe for. But I do it anyway. What choice do I have?

"That's fine," I say quietly, rising from the bed. "I'd rather have you spend the rest of your life hating me for doing everything in my power to keep you safe than spend a single goddamn second existing in a world where I failed to keep you alive, Bella. So long as you're breathing, I can live with you hating me. But the minute I lose you because I wasn't careful enough is the moment I lose *everything* that matters to me."

I lean down and press a kiss to her crown. "You leave this house, there will be hell to pay."

"I'll leave if I want to leave." She turns her face away from me. But not before I see the tears slipping down her cheeks.

Yet again, I've made her cry.

Only I don't regret it this time. Her life matters. It matters a whole helluva lot.

CHAPTER TEN
Bella

"I'm not going to run away if I go to the kitchen," I growl, glaring daggers at Callum. "You can stop following me."

"Who says I'm following you?" He arches a dark brow, leaning back against the door jamb. "Maybe I'm just thirsty."

I huff out a breath, not buying that for a minute. He's been stalking me all over the house since he got here five minutes before Cormac left. It's driving me crazy. I can't think with him acting like my shadow.

A tiny part of me wants to make a break for it and see how far I can get. Not because I think I'll actually get anywhere. But just to make him sweat. It's his own fault, really. He's mildly infuriating.

"Does the Army train you to be a pain in the ass, or does that come naturally?" I ask, plopping down at the island.

Crash settles at my feet, shooting Callum a reproachful look. At least he's on my side.

"Oh, it's a natural talent, sweetheart."

I crack a smile, my first since Cormac left an hour ago. I'm freaking miserable without him. I'm worried out of my mind for Isla. I feel helpless because there's nothing I can do. And I'm sad because I acted like a brat and didn't say bye. I'm also mad as hell that he threatened to tie me to the bed.

It hurts that he doesn't trust me...and it hurts even more that I didn't give him any reason to trust me today. Callum is here because I made Cormac think the worst. I reacted instead of trying to see things from his point of view.

He *needs* me safe, not because I'm a job. Not because he promised my dad. But because he loves me. If something happens to me, it will destroy him. The same damn way thinking about losing him destroys me.

I don't hate him for that. How can I when my heart beats for him?

But that doesn't mean he can just order me around, either. He has to talk to me, not go all bossy caveman on me. I've never responded well to being bossed around. Just ask Isla. She's older than me by a couple of minutes and has spent twenty-one years being bossy. I've spent just as long being stubborn and recalcitrant. I think these traits were forged in my soul in the womb.

"If you're going to be a weirdo and follow me around, can you at least sit down?" I complain to Callum, nudging a barstool toward him. "You're making me nuts."

"Pretty sure I had nothing to do with that," he mutters without heat, making me laugh. He's growing on me. Sort of like a wart. Only he's more attractive and slightly less annoying.

"I'm perfectly sane."

He snorts, hooking his foot around the barstool to drag it across the floor. Once it's positioned so he can see both doors, he sits, his back ramrod straight.

"How long were you in the Army?"

"Long enough."

"Did you like it?"

"No one likes the Army, Bella."

"Oh."

"He's going to find your sister."

Tears sting my eyes. I fidget with my hands, twisting my fingers together.

"I know," I whisper. Cormac *will* find her. He's never let me down. I know he won't this time, either.

Isla has always been the twin who follows the rules and never makes waves. She tries to make everyone else happy, even if it means sacrificing her own joy. For her to sneak out now is serious.

I wish I knew what was going on with her. What is she hiding? Why didn't she talk to me about whatever it is? I don't like that she has a secret. We tell each other everything.

I heave a sigh, giving up on trying to sort it out. "Are you hungry?" I ask Callum.

He eyes me sideways.

"I'm making eggs. I promise not to poison them if you promise to at least let me pee in peace today."

"I'll cook."

I gape at him.

"And you can still pee in peace."

"Jerk," I mumble, fighting a smile.

He grins at me.

Crash lifts his head, growling.

"I'll give you eggs, too, buddy," I promise, laughing. He's getting a little spoiled.

He ignores me and jumps to his feet, his hackles rising. I watch, not understanding as he starts to pace in restless circles, barking and growling.

"Crash?"

A hint of wood smoke wafts toward me, seeming to come from nowhere.

"Bella."

I jerk my gaze up to Callum, his sharp tone cutting through the confusion in my mind.

"Take my cell and go to the panic room," he orders me, his face a grim mask. He smells it too.

Cold dread sinks its claws in deep, turning my blood to ice. Something is wrong. Seriously wrong.

"Go," he says, shoving his phone into my hand. "Call 911, then call Cormac."

"Callum," I whisper, shaking as he pulls a gun from his waistband.

"Go," he growls.

I bolt down the hall, terror pounding like the strike of a gong in my chest. Crash follows behind me, still growling. I run into Cormac's office, heading straight for the closet.

As soon as I'm inside the panic room, I set the phone down and heave the door closed before cranking the wheel to lock it into place. It works like a bank vault. There is no opening it from the other side without the code.

The panic room is small but comfortable. It's bullet-proof, fireproof, tamper proof. If someone is out there, they aren't getting inside, not without a whole lot of time and equipment.

I grab Callum's phone from the floor and scurry to the small sofa. Crash climbs up with me, as if sensing that I need him close. I wrap one arm around his body, trying not to sob as I hit the button to light up Callum's screen.

He doesn't have a lock on the phone.

It takes three tries before I manage to dial 911.

"I need help!" I cry as soon as the dispatcher answers. "I think someone is on the property, trying to burn the house down."

"I understand, ma'am. What's the address?"

My heart sinks. Cormac told me everything from codes to the panic rooms to the lock on the gun safe, but the giant jerk forgot to give me the address.

"I don't know," I sob, trying to remember the numbers on the mailbox. "221 County Road 74, I think. It's Cormac Carmichael's house."

"Okay, good," the dispatcher says. "That's good. We know the place. What's your name?"

"Bella."

"Can you tell me what happened, Bella?"

"I witnessed a murder back home. Now someone is on the property and Cormac isn't here."

"You're there alone?"

"Callum," I rasp. "Callum is here."

"Good." The dispatcher sounds relieved. Does everyone know everyone in this town? "Are you in a safe room, Bella?"

I guess everyone *does* know everyone if he knows about the panic rooms.

"Yes. On the bottom floor."

"Good. I want you to stay there until the fire department gets there. The panic room is fireproof. You'll be safe in there. Don't come out until I tell you that you can."

"I have to call Cormac."

"I need you to stay on the phone with me, Bella."

"I'm sorry," I whisper and then disconnect. It's the last thing I should do, I know that, but if I die, I don't want the last words between me and Cormac to be the ones we spoke this morning. I want him to know that I love him and that I'm sorry. I'm so damn sorry.

Chapter Eleven
Giant

"Are we getting this fucking plane in the air today or not?" I demand, scowling at Andreas as soon as he emerges from the cockpit.

"Jesus," Hacker mutters beneath his breath, leaning his head back against his seat. "Wake me up when he's done bitching."

I flip him off even though he can't see it. It doesn't make me feel any better. My mood is pitch fucking black. As soon as I left the house, I regretted threatening to tie Bella to the bed. She's independent and strong-willed, and fearless. And she loves her twin fiercely.

Of course she wants to help look for her. Of course she's worried about her. I owed her understanding and patience. That's what she needed from me. Instead, I barked orders and told her what to do.

Like an asshole, I put my needs above hers. She needed me to talk to her. She needed me to give her a voice. Instead, I decided for her. Just like Mac did when he sent her here.

That worked out real well for him, now didn't it?

"The wind had us grounded," Andreas says calmly. "But it's died down now. It shouldn't be much longer before we get clearance to fly."

"About fucking time," I mutter.

Andreas purses his lips, staring at me.

"What?"

"You still have time to call her and apologize for whatever you did," he says, sliding into the seat across from mine.

"What makes you think I did anything?"

Hacker snorts.

Andreas gives me a look that screams cut the bullshit. "I know you," he says. "You're only this goddamn grouchy because you're mad at yourself. So stop being a fucking idiot and fix it already."

I huff a curse, turning to glance out at the tarmac. The Silver Spoon Falls airport is minuscule, but it's a helluva lot closer than any airport in Houston. "What if I can't fix it?"

What if I fucked everything up?

Jesus. I can't even think about it. I told her I could live with her hating me, but that was a fucking lie. It's been an hour, and I feel like I'm losing my mind. I won't survive a week without her, let alone a lifetime. She's in my blood now, pumping through my veins with every beat of my heart.

I need her like air, like water. Like laughter. She's my goddamn soul.

"When the fuck has that ever stopped you?" Andreas asks.

I look back at him.

"You fuck shit up beyond repair at least once a week."

"Twice," Hacker says, eyes still closed.

"Twice," Andreas says, adjusting his estimate. They're both assholes. "And you fix it anyway. It's what you do. You're a fucking bull in a china shop. You bulldoze over everything that gets in your way, and then you fix it. This time matters more than most because you love her, so you'll fix it. You won't be able to settle your overgrown ass down until you fix it."

"What he said," Hacker agrees. "So put us all out of our misery and call her already because you're stressing me the hell out. And this flight hasn't even left the damn ground."

"I didn't ask the two of you to come," I remind them.

"We're ride or die, motherfucker." Andreas grins. "We ride until we die."

"What he said." Hacker cracks one eye open. "Out of curiosity. Do you think you'll have a ring on her finger before she's pregnant?"

"Why?"

"No reason," he lies.

"You shady motherfuckers. Are you betting on whether she's pregnant before we're married?" I growl.

Andreas wipes invisible lint off his jacket, avoiding my gaze.

Hacker shrugs.

The assholes.

"I'm not dignifying that with an answer," I mutter and then pause. "But if I did, I'd bet that she's pregnant first."

Hacker grins, leaning back in his seat again.

Andreas just shakes his head.

I drag my phone out of my pocket, bringing it out of airplane mode to call Mischief and fix what I fucked up. As soon as it registers service, the goddamn thing starts blowing up.

"What the fuck?" I mutter as missed call after missed call rolls in. And then I see the text from Cash, and my entire fucking world stops spinning.

Get home now. Someone set your house on fire and Bella is still inside.

I bellow a curse, jumping up from my seat as rage and terror hit me like a fist.

No. Please, God, no. Not Bella. Not my Mischief.

Hacker jumps.

"We have to go. Now!" I roar, already racing down the aisle. "Someone set my fucking house on fire. Bella is still inside."

Andreas curses.

He and Hacker don't ask a single question. They just hit their feet running.

"Jesus Christ," Andreas whispers.

I make a strangled sound in the back of my throat, wheezing for breath as I try to comprehend the scene outside my gate. An entire half-block is cordoned off, with police cruisers and fire trucks blocking the roadway. Smoke still billows through the trees, a thick, black cloud of it slowly choking the hope out of me.

Hacker pulls his truck as close as he can. I launch myself out before he even stops. I can't breathe. I can't think. This is hell. Literal hell.

"Bella!" I roar, racing for the gate.

"Giant," Dillon Armstrong says, grabbing me by the arm before I can duck beneath the barrier.

I shake him off, a menacing growl ripping from my lips. He isn't stopping me. I don't care if he is the Sheriff and a friend. He isn't stopping me.

"Stop," he says, his voice soft.

My heart cracks, cleaving in two.

"Tell me you have her," I rasp, grabbing him by the vest. "Tell me you have her." I'm not sure if I'm asking, demanding, or begging. "Tell me."

"Cormac."

I let go of Dillon, spinning around so fast I nearly lose my balance. Am I seeing things, or is it her?

"Mischief," I whisper. Soot stains her right cheek and her clothes. Someone wrapped her in a blanket. Crash paces at her side, sticking close.

"You really gotta learn to answer your phone when a girl is having an emergency, Tiny," she says.

I bellow like a wounded fucking bear.

Her blanket flutters to the ground as she launches herself at me, her expression crumbling. Tears pour down her face in a flood as I drag her into my arms.

She's safe.

Ah, God. She's safe.

"They knew where she was going before she ever left the state," Callum says, eyeing me wearily from across the table in the clubhouse kitchen. "They planted a bug at her dad's house."

"Jesus," Cash mutters.

"I'll take care of it," Hacker says, shooting me a look.

I jerk my chin in a nod. The last thing Mac needs is the fucking Dixie Mafia having a hotline directly into his home. He's a billionaire. God only knows what they'd do with access to a man like him and his business partners.

"They were just waiting for an opportunity to make a play for her." Callum fingers the bruise across the side of his face, a savage grin dancing at his lips. "The little fucker said they thought I'd be easier to take down than you."

They won't make that mistake again. He killed one of the two. The other, the little fucker, will be extradited back to Tennessee on murder charges once he's released from the hospital.

It'll be a hot minute before that happens. Callum worked him over good, trying to find out what they knew about Isla. Either he's a better liar than he is a criminal, or he and his buddies know nothing about Mischief's twin.

Whatever Isla is up to has nothing to do with this shit-show. Hacker and Callum are leaving first thing in the morning to help Mac find her, but Mischief's nightmare is over.

I think mine is only just beginning. It'll be a long god-damn time before I forget the abject terror I felt today. I thought I lost her. For several agonizing moments, I thought she was gone. That feeling will haunt me for the rest of my life.

"Are we done here?" I rasp, standing up abruptly. I don't want to be here right now, rehashing what happened today with my MC brothers and my cousin. I don't give a fuck how much damage there is to the house or how long it'll take to repair it. None of that matters. I need to be with Mischief.

"Yeah, brother," Cash says, empathy in his eyes. The same reflects in the face of every single one of our broth-ers— Hands, Cowboy, Andreas, Bender, Fifth, Lynch, Hacker, and Angel. "Go be with your girl. We'll handle shit from here."

I jerk my chin in a nod, grateful beyond measure for the bonds of this brotherhood and the kinship that comes with it. I don't have to explain, not to them. And I don't have to ask, not of them. They know because they've all been here in their own way. We've all hoisted the load so each of us could put it down for a while.

It's who we are. It's what we do. That's the Silver Spoon MC.

"Thank you," I rasp, tapping my hand over my heart.

To a man, they all tap back.

CHAPTER TWELVE

Bella

Cormac's suite at the clubhouse is nothing like I expected. Then again, nothing about him is what I expected. He defies all my expectations in the best ways possible. The heavy driftwood furniture and blue walls make the room feel like an oasis.

I'm seated in the middle of his massive bed, trying to comb through my hair, when he comes barging into the room like he expects to find me crawling out the window. As soon as his gaze settles on me, the tension in his shoulders eases. He closes the door, leaning back against it.

"You showered."

"I smelled like smoke," I say, grimacing. I still can't believe they set his house on fire. Thank God for Crash. Had he not alerted us to danger, we might not have known anyone was on the property until it was too late.

But thanks to his sharp senses, Callum caught them in the act. The living room sustained heavy damage, but the rest of the house is okay. So are we. Well, mostly. Callum is a little banged up and it may be a long time before I sleep peacefully again. But we're safe.

And the monsters who killed Bellamy...well, the one who shot him won't be able to hurt anyone ever again. His accomplice will face the justice system for both of them. I hope he rots in prison. It's better than he deserves.

"I would have showered with you," Cormac says, strolling toward me.

"You were busy."

His handsome face falls into a frown. "I'm never too busy for you, Mischief. I was trying to give you a little space to talk to your parents."

"I know." I tip my head back, staring up at him. Our conversation was emotional. I've never seen my dad tear up like he did today. It made me cry to realize just how worried he's been about me. "Um, they heard from Isla."

"Yeah?"

"She got married. To Bellamy's son, Brantley."

Cormac's eyes widen, but he doesn't seem surprised, not really.

"You guessed, didn't you?"

"I suspected a man was involved, though not which man." He reaches out, twisting one of my curls around his finger. "Girls like your sister don't run away from home in the middle of a crisis unless they have a reason. She's not into drugs, gambling, or anything shady, so that narrows the options."

"I didn't even know she was dating anyone."

"Maybe she didn't think you'd approve," he suggests.

"I..." I heave a sigh. Is that why she didn't tell me? Because she didn't think I'd approve? I haven't exactly been Brantley's biggest fan. I was convinced he was the one who owed money, and I refused to believe anything else. But as I'm quickly coming to learn, people aren't always what you think. The man in front of me is a perfect example of that. He's so much more than I expected.

Maybe Bellamy is another example. He was a good man and a great boss. But that doesn't mean he can't also have been this other thing too. It doesn't mean that he didn't have skeletons in his closet. It doesn't mean his son is to blame for what happened to him. He didn't deserve it. I'll never believe that. But that doesn't mean it wasn't his addiction that started the ball rolling down the hill. It doesn't make Brantley the bad guy.

If Isla loves him, it's because he's someone worth loving.

"I wouldn't have approved," I admit. "But I think maybe I was wrong." I bite my lip, meeting his gaze. "I was wrong today, too, you know."

He watches me intently, not saying anything.

"Even before I thought I might...die," I say, hating the way he flinches when I say the word. "Even before then, I regretted how we left things this morning, Cormac. I was angry, but I didn't mean what I said about never forgiving you."

"I thought I lost you."

"I know," I whisper, feeling two inches tall.

"No. I mean, even before those motherfuckers showed up, I thought I lost you." He expels a breath, sinking to his knees in front of me. "I told you that I could live with you hating me, but it was a fucking lie, Mischief. I don't just need you safe. I need *you*, period."

"I need you too," I whisper, tears slipping down my cheeks. "I was so damn scared I wouldn't get to say I'm sorry for being a brat." My bottom lip quivers, his face blurring. "I thought the last thing you'd ever hear from me was me threatening to never forgive you."

"Don't cry, Mischief. You know it breaks my heart," he croons, cupping my face between his palms. "You're too damn perfect for tears."

"I love you. That's what I wanted you to hear last, Cormac," I say, crawling toward him and then climbing off the bed into his arms.

He pulls me down onto his lap, holding me tightly. I press my lips to his jaw, his cheek, and the corner of his mouth, punctuating each kiss with the same three words.

"I love you. Even when I was angry, I loved you. I'll never stop, Cormac. Not ever."

"Bella," he rumbles, his voice shaking with raw emotion. There's a warning in there, a quiet plea. But I don't heed it.

I don't think he wants me to, anyway. This man loves me best when I'm defying him. It's what I was built to do.

"I love you," I say again. "No matter how bossy you get or how many times you threaten to tie me to the bed to get your way, I'm going to keep loving you."

He growls my name this time, his hands tightening on me as he draws me closer. My shirt slides up my body, dragged higher as his composure slips. I feel his palm against my bare skin and marvel in his warmth, in his touch. In how he can be so discomposed and so controlled at the same time.

"I love–"

He cuts me off with his mouth on mine, stealing my confession. He kisses it from my lips, and then kisses the breath from my lungs. He doesn't let up until dots swim in my field of vision and I'm swaying in his arms, caught between the desperate need to kiss him forever and the burning need to breathe.

"It's my turn now, little girl," he says, peeling my shirt off my body as he rises to his feet. He flings it to the floor, tumbling me backwards onto the bed. His hard body covers mine, pinning me beneath him.

I wrap myself around him, sighing his name in bliss.

"You're my soul," he growls, kissing all over my neck. "I know love because of you. I feel joy because you're mine. Every damn beat of my heart is for you, Bella."

"Cormac," I breathe, dragging his shirt up his body. He pulls away long enough to rip it off over his head and then he's back, his bare skin against mine.

We work together, our hands sliding against one another's as we attack his pants, trying to get them undone. As soon as he frees his cock, it's in my hands.

"Fuck," he groans, his head kicked back. Hot possession pours like water from his gunmetal gray eyes, drenching me.

"I need you."

"You have me. You have every piece of me, baby." He tips his head forward, his expression so damn serious. "You'll always have every piece of me."

"I need you in me," I clarify.

"Have I had my snack yet, Mischief? No. So settle your little ass down and stop rushing me," he growls, prowling down my body.

I don't bother telling him not to rip my leggings. He's just going to do it anyway.

Right on cue, he tears the crotch out of them.

"What the fuck?" His head snaps up, his eyes meeting mine. "Where are your panties?"

"Don't have them. Don't miss them. Would skip them again," I say, smiling sweetly.

His scowl is black enough to frighten the devil. Luckily, I don't scare easily.

"Oh, Mischief," he growls, that pirate smile overtaking his face. "I'm going to have fun with you."

"Get on with it then."

The next thing I know, I'm face down on the bed with his hand on my ass. I yelp and then moan as the sting bleeds to pleasure.

He hauls me right back up, flipping us so he's on his back beneath me, and I'm straddling his face.

"Take a seat," he growls.

Oh, my.

I gently lower myself down, but he's not having any of that.

"I said sit your little ass down, baby. Now, grab a pillow and cover that sassy mouth."

"What? Why...?"

He smacks my ass again and yanks me down onto his mouth.

I grab a pillow, shoving my face into it just in time to muffle my shout. He doesn't eat me. He freaking sends me catapulting through the sky like a meteor.

I sob into the pillow, rocking my hips against his face as he eats me alive, drowning me in bliss. I come within seconds, but he doesn't stop. He just grabs me around the waist and keeps going.

I scream his name, bucking my hips, grinding against his tongue, praying for him to have mercy and to never stop.

The second orgasm hits with the force of an atomic bomb. And all I can do is take it. It's heaven and it's hell, my own personal paradise.

Cormac flips me onto my back, rolling on top of me. He pries the pillow from my grip, those eyes still full of deadly possession. "You wear panties around other men, Mischief," he growls, leaning down so his lips are a mere breath from mine. "Or you'll be walking around dripping my cum morning, noon, and night."

"Cormac," I whimper.

"Fuck. It's impossible to be mad at you when you sound so sweet saying my name like that." He brushes my hair back from my face, brushing his lips against mine in a gentle kiss. "Who am I kidding? It's impossible to be mad at you when you own my whole goddamn heart."

"Make love to me."

He drags my leg up over his hip, tangling our hands together.

We both moan as he pushes his way inside me, slowly stretching me. His hips come to rest against mine, and once again, I know what it is to be complete.

"I love you, Mischief," he breathes. "Fuck, how I love you, little girl."

"Show me," I demand.

He does. With his body covering mine, with his lips, and hands, and whole heart, he does.

"Marry me," he whispers hours later, holding me close. "Stay right here in Silver Spoon Falls and build a future with me, Mischief."

My breath stalls in my throat. I flip around in the bed to face him. "Do you mean it? You want to marry me?"

He smiles, stroking his finger down my nose. "I even asked Mac for permission. Mostly."

"Mostly?" I give him a look.

"Okay, I told him that I'm marrying you and he needs to give us his damn blessing to make you happy and shit." Those dimples pop out, wicked humor dancing in his eyes. "Frankly, Mischief, the fact that I said anything before marrying you makes me his favorite son-in-law right now."

"Cormac!"

He chuckles. "I'm just kidding, baby. I asked his permission. I even let him threaten my life and my cock."

I groan, burying my face against his shoulder.

"Are you going to say yes?"

"I'm trying to decide," I tease. "Does this proposal come with a ring?"

"Yes, but no."

"Yes, but no? I wonder about your sanity sometimes, Tiny."

"Shit, me too." He laughs. "You have a ring, Mischief. But Dillon is a dick. He wouldn't let me back in the house to get it."

"What does it look like?" I ask. Truthfully, it could have come from a Cracker Jack's box, and my answer would still be the same. But if I don't torture him a little bit, I'm not doing my job.

"It's purple, he says. "And it vibrates."

"It vibrates?"

He waggles his brows suggestively.

I smack him with a pillow, making him laugh.

"Stop fucking with me and say yes, Bella," he growls, wrestling the pillow away and then pinning me beneath him. "Marry me."

"Oh, I suppose I'll marry you," I say, feigning boredom as I wrap my arms around his neck. "I mean since your magic water brought me here and everything."

"Fuck yeah, it did," he breathes against my lips. "I swam naked in it and everything."

I bury my face in his throat to muffle my laughter. God, I love this crazy man.

Epilogue

Giant

"I have a plan."

A chorus of groans sounds from all edges of the yard where my brothers are laid out like they're dying.

"Fuck you and your plans, brother," Andreas growls, lifting his head to look at me from his position on the ground. The way he's laid out, you'd think the fucker just ran a marathon.

"Agreed," Hacker grunts, tossing a wrench aside. "No offense, but your plans are fucking terrible."

"I'm pretty goddamn sure all of this was his idea," Cowboy mutters, grabbing a bottle of water from the cooler the girls hauled outside an hour ago. He drags the back of his arm across his forehead, cursing beneath his breath. "I'm too old for this shit."

"You're younger than I am." Cash rolls his eyes at Cowboy and then grimaces, twisting like he's trying to work kinks out of his lower back. "I think I broke my ass."

"Aww. Did Hadley spank you too hard last night?" I ask, grinning at him.

Hands cracks a smile, chuckling.

"Man, fuck you." Cash laughs. "I'm serious. I pulled something in my ass trying to wrestle that goddamn slide into place."

"Why the fuck didn't we hire professionals for this shit?" Lynch shields his eyes, looking up at us from a prone position on the ground beside Andreas.

Every single one of my brothers turns to look at him with matching expressions.

"Motherfucker, you are a professional." I kick his boot. "At least that's what you've been trying to tell us for the last two decades."

He scowls at me. "Not even a goddamn engineer is qualified to build your Wish version of a playground, Giant."

"He's not wrong," Angel mutters.

Fifth snorts his agreement, leaning back against a shade tree with his eyes closed.

"First of all, fuckers," I growl, "this shit didn't come from Wish. It's state-of-the-art." There's not a chance in hell I'd risk my girls' safety on anything less than the absolute best equipment on the market. My girls are worth every damn penny I spent, too. "Second, if you'd quit bitching for two minutes, I said I have a plan."

"Hurry up with it then," Bender growls. "If I sweat anymore, my goddamn balls are going to chafe."

"We send our wives shopping and call reinforcements," I mutter, nodding to the group of women lined up in lounge chairs on the far side of the yard. As soon as they heard we were going to be building things, they suddenly all decided they needed tans. Never mind the fact that Bella hasn't tanned in the entire six years we've been married.

I'm almost positive none of the others have either. They're here to watch the show. Not that they're getting much of one at this point. It's one-hundred damn degrees out, and building an entire playground for the kids is a goddamn nightmare.

We're all too old for this shit. Luckily, we have friends and an entire crop of brothers who aren't here today. And those friends and brothers owe us favors. There's no labor like free labor.

"I take back everything I said," Andreas mutters. "Your plan is golden."

"What's that?" I cup my hand around my ear. "I didn't quite catch that."

"He said you aren't nearly as idiotic as that big ass head makes you look," Hands says, grinning at me.

I laugh, flipping him the bird.

A sharp whistle cuts through the air, followed by, "Hey, Tiny!"

I lift my gaze, glancing toward the row of loungers on the far side of the yard to find my wife standing a few feet in front of hers, her hands planted on her wide hips.

"Less talking! More sweating!" she shouts. "You're ruining our view."

A ripple of laughter moves through the row of loungers.

"We want to see muscles!" Catriona shouts.

"And sweat!" cries Hadley.

I glance at my brothers to find them glancing at each other, matching looks on their faces. We don't discuss it. We don't say anything. Everyone jumps up with renewed purpose, leaving our tools where they lay.

I stalk toward Mischief, rapidly closing the distance between us.

"What are you doing?" she asks warily.

"Giving you what you asked for," I say conversationally. "What was it again?"

"I don't remember," she lies, inching backward as if she has a shot in hell of getting away from me. She's been trying to outrun me for six years, and it hasn't worked yet. I always catch her little ass. And she always loves it when I do.

Life with her and our twin daughters is a goddamn adventure. The most incredible, beautiful adventure I've ever experienced. And somehow, she keeps finding ways to make it better.

I don't merely love this woman. I idolize her. She's not simply the center of my universe. She's every damn corner of it. I'm not just happy with her. I'm fucking ecstatic. Every day, I know joy. I know bliss. I know my purpose.

"Ah, yes," I say. "It was muscles. And sweat."

"Tiny," she says, a warning in her voice. I don't heed it. Of course I don't.

She feints left, and I break right, catching her before she even makes it two steps. I haul her into my arms, being mindful of her pregnant belly, and then shove my face into hers.

"I believe you said something about a view too," I growl.

"Damn," she breathes as squeals go up all around us from my brothers' wives. Her arms lock around my neck. "What a view."

I chuckle. "That's my line, Mischief. You're the view."

"Not today, Tiny," she sighs happily, dragging my mouth down to hers. "Not today."

Author's Note

If you enjoyed The Bodyguard, please consider leaving a review! I appreciate them so much!

Not ready to leave the Silver Spoon MC clubhouse in the rearview? Me either! All five of my Silver Spoon MC stories will be available in an ebook and paperback bundle (with bonus content!) on January 4th in the Silver Spoon MC Collection: Nichole's Crew! Loni's will be available on the same date!

Xavier's Kitten (Tate's brother), Snow's Prince (Devin's brother) , Callum's Hope (Giant's cousin), and Aurora's Knight (Devin's former bodyguard) are also coming to Silver Spoon Falls January through April of 2023!

SILVER SPOON MC

These wealthy Texans have it all—Money, looks, power, their MC, and brothers. The only thing missing is someone to share it all with. There's a shortage of eligible ladies in town but these determined men won't let that slow them down. These MC brothers are going to turn the town of Silver Spoon Falls, Texas, on its ear looking for their curvy soulmates.

Beginning in February 2022, Nichole Rose and Loni Ree are bringing you the Silver Spoon MC Series and these aren't your typical MC romance stories. Nichole and Loni like to keep things light. Come along with us on this wild instalove ride.

The CEO by Loni Ree - February 4, 2022
http://mybook.to/TheCEOLoniRee
The Surgeon by Nichole Rose - March 1, 2022
http://mybook.to/TheSurgeon
The Cowboy by Loni Ree - April 4, 2022 -
https://books2read.com/TheCowboyLoniRee
The Heir by Nichole Rose - May 3, 2022 -
http://mybook.to/TheHeirNR
The Rockstar by Loni Ree - June 10, 2022
https://books2read.com/TheRockstar
The Lawyer by Nichole Rose - July 5, 2022
http://mybook.to/TheLawyerNR
The Architect by Loni Ree- August 5, 2022
books2read.com/TheArchitectLoniRee
The Prodigy by Nichole Rose- September 6, 2022
http://mybook.to/TheProdigyNR
The Prince by Loni Ree - October 7, 2022
https://books2read.com/ThePrinceLoniRee
The Bodyguard by Nichole Rose- November 1, 2022
http://mybook.to/TheBodyguardNR

ICE GIANT

This hockey player is ready for war on and off the ice. Let the games begin!

Jonas Michaud

There are two places I'm not supposed to be: in trouble and in a gentleman's club.

But thanks to my sister, I find myself in both anyway.

And just in time to rescue the sports reporter who drives me crazy.

Jamie Knight is the curviest little enemy I've ever had.

She's been publishing stories about my hockey teammates for years.

But I want her attention focused on me.

Finding me in Dionysus is the story of her career.

Imagine my surprise when it never airs.

She's determined to keep her secrets.

I intend to uncover every single one.

And I have no intention of backing down until she's mine.

Jamie Knight

There are two things I did not expect: being propositioned in a dungeon or being saved by the hockey player of my dreams.

But thanks to my best friend, here I am anyway.

I only came to Dionysus to get a peek at Nashville's naughtiest.

Instead, I'm leaving with the story of my lifetime.

But I've been in love with Jonas Michaud and his wild ways since I set eyes on him.

Airing this story would destroy him, and that's the last thing I want to do.

So I keep his secret.

I did not expect him to declare war on my traitorous body to find out why.

He knows my deepest desires now.

And this ice giant has every intention of using them to make me melt.

When this giant sets his sights on his curvy girl, nothing will stop him from claiming her. If you enjoy OTT possessive hockey players, curvy heroines, and steamy instalove romance, you'll love this naughty Canadian and his favorite little enemy.

Ice Giant releases on November 15th! Find it here!

Instalove Book Club

The Instalove Book Club is now in session!

Get the inside scoop from your favorite instalove authors, meet new authors to love, and snag freebies and bonus content from featured authors every month. The Instalove Book Club newsletter goes out once per week!

Join now to get your hands on bonus scenes and brand-new, exclusive content from our first six featured authors.

Join the Club: http://instalovebookclub.com

NICHOLE'S BOOK BEAUTIES

Want to connect with Nichole and other readers? We're building a girl gang! Join Nichole Rose's Book Beauties on Facebook for fun, games, and behind-the-scenes exclusives!

FOLLOW NICHOLE

Sign-up for Nichole's mailing list at http://authornic holerose.com/newsletter to stay up to date on all new releases and for exclusive ARC giveaways from Nichole Rose.

Want to connect with Nichole and other readers? Join Nichole Rose's Book Beauties on Facebook!

facebook.com/AuthorNicholeRose/

instagram.com/AuthorNicholeRose

twitter.com/AuthNicholeRose

bookbub.com/authors/nichole-rose

tiktok.com/@authornicholerose

MORE BY NICHOLE ROSE

Her Alpha Series

Her Alpha Daddy Next Door

Her Alpha Boss Undercover

Her Alpha's Secret Baby

Her Alpha Protector

Her Date with an Alpha

Her Alpha: The Complete Series

Her Bride Series

His Future Bride

His Stolen Bride

His Secret Bride

His Curvy Bride

His Captive Bride

His Blushing Bride

His Bride: The Complete Series

Claimed Series

Possessing Liberty

Teaching Rowan

Claiming Caroline

Kissing Kennedy

Claimed: The Complete Series

Love on the Clock Series

Adore You

Hold You

Keep You

Protect You

Love on the Clock: The Complete Series

The Billionaires' Club

The Billionaire's Big Bold Weakness

The Billionaire's Big Bold Wish

The Billionaire's Big Bold Woman

The Billionaire's Big Bold Wonder

Playing for Keeps

Cutie Pie

Ice Breaker

Ice Prince

Ice Giant (coming soon)

The Second Generation

A Blushing Bride for Christmas

Love Bites

Come Undone

Dripping Pearls

Silver Spoon MC

The Surgeon

The Heir

The Lawyer

The Prodigy

The Bodyguard

Silver Spoon MC Collection - Nichole's Crew

Echoes of Forever

His Christmas Miracle

Taken by the Hitman

Wicked Saint

<u>The Ruined Trilogy</u>
Physical Science
Wrecked

<u>Destination Romance</u>
Romancing the Cowboy
Beach House Beauty

<u>Standalone Titles</u>
A Touch of Summer
Black Velvet
His Secret Obsession
Dirty Boy
Naughty Little Elf
Devil's Deceit
A Bride for the Beast (writing with Fern Fraser)

<u>Easy on Me</u>
Easy Ride
Easy Surrender

One Night with You

Falling Hard

Model Behavior

Learning Curve

Angel Kisses

writing with Loni Ree as Loni Nichole

Dillon's Heart

Razor's Flame

Ryker's Reward (coming soon)

Zane's Rebel (coming soon)

About Nichole Rose

Nichole Rose is a short romance author on the west coast. Her books feature headstrong, sassy women and the alpha males who consume them. From grumpy detectives to country boys with attitude to instalove and over-the-top declarations, nothing is off-limits.

Nichole is sure to have a steamy, sweet story just right for everyone. She fully believes the world is ugly enough without trying to fit falling in love into a one-size-fits-all box. When not writing, Nichole enjoys fine wine, cute shoes, and everything supernatural. She is happily married to the love of her life and is a proud mama to the world's most ridiculous fur-babies.

You can learn more about Nichole and her books at her website .

f

facebook.com/AuthorNicholeRose/

instagram.com/AuthorNicholeRose

twitter.com/AuthNicholeRose

bookbub.com/authors/nichole-rose

tiktok.com/@authornicholerose

www.ingramcontent.com/pod-product-compliance
Lightning Source LLC
Chambersburg PA
CBHW050340160726

48002CB00001B/389